Gabe stared at the b... ...the gym.

"Gabe, you made it! How are you?"

Gabe heard his name and looked all around the gym before he realized that Amy was standing right in front of him, her bangs sticking to her forehead, and her face looking pink and beautiful from the exertion of the game.

"You came to see me!" she blurted out in her shy, excited way. "Oh, thanks. I was hoping you'd come. Wasn't it a good game? I can't wait for Saturday night."

Gabe just nodded, barely letting Amy's words enter further than his ears. He was still fuming over Kat and Brent and the disgusting fact that there was nothing he could do about it.

**Look for this and other books in the
TOTALLY HOT series:**

point

TOTALLY HOT

#2 Breaking Away

Linda A. Cooney

SCHOLASTIC INC.
New York Toronto London Auckland Sydney

ISBN 0-590-44561-8

12 11 10 9 8 7 6 5 4 3 2 1   1 2 3 4 5 6/9

Printed in the U.S.A.   01

First Scholastic printing, October 1991

<u>ONE</u>

Kat McDonough was freezing.

She stood on Miranda's driveway shivering, while rain pelted down. There was water everywhere. It poured from the gutters and ran down the panes of the windows. Beyond Miranda's front deck, waves crashed onto the Crescent Bay beach, shooting up like geysers and giving off weird, iridescent light.

Kat let the rain soak her as she waited in the dark. Her hair was already slicked down. Her big Irish-knit sweater hung from her arms. She had begun to wonder if she was going to wait all night, when Miranda's kitchen door finally opened, and Miranda's father and mother ducked out. They jogged across the driveway with a shared newspaper over their heads and got into their car. Kat shivered once more as the car pulled into the street.

A split second later, the kitchen door flew open again, and Kat's best friend ran out.

"Miranda!"

"Kat!"

"I'm over here."

"Are you sure my parents are gone?" Miranda cried in a hushed, frantic voice. Her long dark hair flapped across her face as she ran down the front steps and across the gravel. Her usual blazer and skirt had been replaced by a man's shirt, a rain slicker, and sweatpants rolled up to the calves. Only her tiny diamond earrings reminded Kat of the controlled, put-together Miranda who was president of their junior class.

"I'm sure they're gone," Kat said.

Miranda hugged Kat, clinging even after Kat let her go. Her hands clutched, and her body trembled.

"Thank you so much for coming," she blurted out. "I'm sorry I couldn't tell you more on the phone. I was afraid my dad would overhear. I'm sorry for fighting with you last weekend. I'm sorry I've barely been able to see you since I left the Turnaround Formal. No one knows what happened to me. I don't want anyone to know, except you."

"I know you've been grounded," Kat assured

her. "I know you haven't been allowed to make phone calls." She tried to guide Miranda back toward the house, away from the beach and the rain, but Miranda wouldn't budge. "I'm not mad at you anymore, anyway. I don't even want to think about last weekend and the Turnaround Formal. It's over."

"But it's not over," Miranda insisted, suddenly moving away from Kat and standing very still, while the rain rushed down her face. "It's not over at all."

Before Kat could ask Miranda what she meant, a boy stepped up from the promenade, the concrete path that separated Miranda's yard from the edge of the beach. He stood and stared at Miranda as if he were a ghost who'd just appeared from the sea. Dark haired, leggy, wearing a leather jacket and carrying a skateboard, he let water run down his face without wiping a single drop away. Kat knew him from school. But she was still confused. He didn't fit with Miranda's house or a late night alone in the dark.

"Kat, it's me, Jackson," he informed her in a strong, assured voice. He took a step closer and set down his skateboard. "Jackson Magruder."

"Jackson?" Kat gasped as the water began to drip off her sweater and soak through her tights.

Jackson was a junior, too, and editor of their school newspaper. Quirky and well respected, he was not one of Kat's and Miranda's tight knit crowd. He was as original and offbeat as Miranda was orderly. Kat had always thought that Jackson and Miranda hated each other.

Instead of explaining, Miranda ran to Jackson. Or maybe he ran to her. Surrounded by wet air and slants of rain, they hugged one another as if they were the last two people on earth. Even through the heavy rain, Kat could see the urgency of their hands, and the care and importance with which they touched each other. Unable to stop themselves, they pressed their mouths together, parting only when Miranda began to cry.

Kat no longer needed an explanation. Now she knew exactly why Miranda had run out of the Turnaround Formal. Rather than be crowned Princess and her Shining Knight with Eric Geraci, the football hero she'd dated for so long, but obviously no longer loved, Miranda had wanted to be with Jackson.

Miranda pulled out of Jackson's kiss, but kept her arms woven around his waist. She was so wet now that her hair hung in heavy strips.

"Jackson met me after I ran out of the formal,"

Miranda explained. "He walked me home. When we finally got back here it was pretty late, but my dad was waiting up."

Kat nodded.

Miranda shuddered. "You know how my dad adores Eric. Well, my father couldn't believe that I deserted Eric at the formal. He blames Jackson, too. He thinks we did a terrible thing."

"What do you want me to do?" Kat asked.

Miranda looked at Jackson, who protectively swept wet hair off the side of her face. "My parents just went down to their country club. I have no idea how long they'll be gone. I know it's horrible out and that I'm asking so much. But you're my best friend and I didn't know who else to ask. Would you keep watch so Jackson and I can at least talk?"

"I won't stay long," Jackson interrupted. "We just need you to warn us in case they come back early. We're going to go down to the beach."

"Will you help us?" Miranda pleaded. "I know I should never have asked you, but I don't know what else to do."

"Of course I'll help," Kat answered.

Miranda gave Kat a grateful smile before embracing Jackson again. Kat looked off at the waves. She really didn't mind standing in the rain. She didn't even mind that Miranda had kept everything a secret. If there was one thing Kat could relate to, it was the feeling of being out of control.

"I can't believe we're finally together."

Miranda and Jackson grasped each other and then tumbled down onto the beach. The rain had turned soft, but the sand was mushy and clung to their clothes, making everything feel grainy and cold. Neither one of them cared. It had been so long, and so hard to get to see each other, that it seemed like a miracle now they were in each other's arms.

"I've missed you so much," Jackson said. "I know it's only been four days, but it feels like forever."

"It feels like forever to me, too." Miranda rested her head on Jackson's warm shoulder. "I can't stand not seeing you."

"Have you told your father that?"

Miranda lifted her head, then shook it slowly as a large wave crashed farther down the beach and the tide quickly ran in. "My father will never change his mind," she said.

"Miranda, no one never changes his mind." Jackson tipped his face up to the rain, rubbed his eyes, then sighed. "Have you tried talking to him about me? I mean, since Saturday night?"

"He said he doesn't want to hear anymore about you. The only boy he thinks I should go out with — "

" — is Eric Geraci," Jackson finished her sentence.

Miranda pulled away from Jackson, hugged her knees and looked down to the ocean. The mix of high waves and low breakers reminded her of what she was feeling inside: how confused it all was, how powerful and risky. She wasn't used to feeling this way, and she didn't know how to handle it. Kat was the emotional one, the one who always threw herself over the edge, whereas Miranda usually had every detail in her life under perfect control. Last summer, when she and Kat had met two out-of-town boys at the amusement park, Miranda had been the one to say: It's late. Enough. Let's go home. Kat was the one who had stayed and fallen in love. And in the end, Kat had been so deeply hurt that Miranda thought she might never recover.

But now, as Miranda looked back at Jackson's drenched, daring face, she wondered if she might be headed for the same end. No. Not with Jackson. Never.

"At least we can meet each other at school," Jackson said in a hurried voice. "I feel like we're playing a game when I walk by you in the hallway and we act like we barely know each other." He knelt on the sand to face her. "Miranda, I run the newspaper. I spend my time making sure that people face reality, not hide from it. If we start out telling people at school that we're together, then maybe later it will be easier to deal with your father."

Miranda stared down at the rolling waves.

"Kat knows," Jackson argued.

"Kat's my best friend, and I didn't tell her until tonight," Miranda came back in a quiet voice.

"Well, tell other people," Jackson insisted. "Don't you have to make a speech before school tomorrow?"

Miranda nodded.

"Most of our class will be there. Why don't I walk you up to the podium?"

Miranda got a seasick feeling inside. She was already terrified about speaking in front of her classmates again. It would be her first appearance before her class since the Turnaround Formal. It was time for the activity announcement she made every month as president of the junior class. The only reason she hadn't asked the class vice president to take over for her was because she'd promised Kat that she would plug a special KHOT show, Kat's program on the campus radio station.

"No," Miranda finally said. "Why don't we meet at lunch instead. We can sneak off campus to that vacant lot you showed me, the one across the street from school."

"Okay. But we can't always be looking over our shoulders," Jackson insisted. "We have to face the world sometime."

"I know," Miranda said quietly, "I know."

"Whoa . . . how wet can a person be?"

Walking home an hour later, Kat turned away from the beach. She caught water that dripped off the end of her nose. She intentionally stepped in puddles. Finally her desert boots were so soaked that she took them off and walked in bare feet. She *was* awfully wet, but she was also preoccupied. Seeing Jackson and Miranda so much in love had reminded her of the times in her life when she'd been carried away, too.

"Unfortunately, it's never over some decent guy like Jackson, or even Eric Geraci," she told herself as she strode back. Even Gabe Sachs, her just-friend partner at the radio station, was a much better person than the guys she fell for.

"I need some kind of jerk radar detector," Kat whispered. "One that works every time."

Kat wasn't just remembering last summer. Not that she would ever forget Grady Howard, an out-of-town boy who she'd met at the old amusement park down by the pier. Kat and Grady had made love, Kat's one and only time. Then the next day, he'd gone home to Santa Cruz. After that, despite a promise that he would call, write, or visit, he'd never even returned her autographed Lily Tomlin book.

But the worst part was that Grady had just been the most serious blunder in a long line of dumb mistakes. When it came to guys, Kat had two speeds. Stop and full steam ahead. When she fell for someone, she didn't think, she just plunged in. That was how she'd ended up with Steven Casalini, who'd stood Kat up for the middle school prom, Lewis Vandenberg, who'd gotten drunk and tried to drive her father's car, and Sean Smith, who had flirted with her only to try and get to know Miranda. It was no wonder that after Grady, Kat had decided that the only solution was to clamp down her feelings and stuff them into a place where they only came out as routines and jokes.

"That's me," Kat chattered, turning off the prom and starting up Twelfth Street, past the Sea Bee Motel and the Surf Shop. She swung her desert boots by the laces. "Smart and funny, a joke a minute, always ready for the witty comeback — unless I fall for some guy, in which case I just throw my brain and my wits into the trash can and walk around with my heart in the middle of my forehead."

Hopping from the curb to gutter, curb to gutter as if she were doing a folk dance, Kat decided to entertain herself with a comic monologue. She turned onto Bayview Lane and approached the big Victorian house her parents had converted to a bed and breakfast inn.

"The story of Kat McDonough's love life," she babbled. "See, I decided to take one last chance for some insane reason," she chattered, "jump in, get my bare feet wet — I like to use swimming imagery, since I'm on the swim team — anyway, I asked this guy to the Turn-around Formal — not just *any* guy — Brent Tucker, the newest, richest, smartest, most gorgeous, etcetera, etcetera . . ." She stepped on a rock, then hobbled. "Hey, I don't fool around and I never do things half way. When I jump, I *jump*. So anyway, I thought Brent was great. Until the ungreat part at the end of the formal, when I caught him kissing Lisa Avery, the sexiest, most infuriating senior girl at my school." She slapped her soggy thigh. "Now *that* was a laugh riot!"

But when Kat crossed the street and looked into the rain again, her sense of humor fled.

"Oh, no."

A red BMW was parked under her magnolia tree. Kat only knew of one spiffy new car like that, and as she crept closer she saw the personalized California plate. *TUCKER.* Then she spotted Brent, sitting on her porch steps with his head in his hands. His head was bowed gracefully. She wondered if he'd heard her talking to herself and prayed that the sound of the rain had drowned her out.

"What is he doing here?" she whispered as she slowly walked up the brick path.

Brent looked up. His hair was dry, and flopped, silky and golden, over his forehead. He wore a hooded field jacket with pockets and flaps, pleated pants, pressed white shirt, and loafers with no socks. He didn't move. For a moment she thought he would just sit there like that while she trudged right past him and went on into her house.

Kat kept walking, her feet like two lumps of mud, her limbs feeling like she was moving in slow motion. He still didn't look at her. It wasn't until she reached for the door that she felt his hand grasp her wet, bare foot.

"You're cold," Brent said in a concerned voice. "Don't you believe in putting on shoes?"

"What's the point?" she joked, trying to act like she didn't care. "I'd just take them off again."

"Ha, ha," he responded, without humor.

Kat's teeth began to chatter. She told herself to just go into the house, to shut the door on him, but she couldn't get her feet to take that final step. Finally, she leaned her forehead against the front door. When she looked down she saw the bright bunch of flowers lying on the step, next to Brent's left hand. So what, she told herself. So he'd bought flowers. Money meant nothing to Brent. His parents owned the fancy new Tucker Resort.

Brent still held onto her foot. "You're avoiding me at school. How can I prove myself to you if you don't give me a chance?"

"You proved yourself at the Turnaround Formal," she said flatly.

"I told you, it wasn't my fault! How can I prove that to you? Write on the walls of the gym? Have the principal announce it over the intercom?"

"You could start there," she cracked.

Then he leaned forward, and for a second Kat had the crazy impression that he was going to kiss her foot.

But he didn't. He just bent over to pick up the flowers. Then he stood up and handed them to her. For the first time that night, she was faced with the full impact of his soulful blue eyes, his lean, elegant face. He looked at her as the rain came down.

"Whatever it takes," he finally said, "I'll do it."

Only when Kat took his flowers and breathed in their spicy perfume did Brent stick his hands in his pockets and slowly walk back to his car.

TWO

When Miranda arrived early at school the next morning, ready to give her activity report, she couldn't get the image of a prison out of her head.

Every morning she would open her eyes and see lines of foggy gray light coming through the mini-blinds above her bed. *Bars.* She would hear the busy footsteps of her mother and father pacing along the hardwood floors, getting ready for work. *Guards.* She would finally march downstairs, and see the note her father had plastered over the telephone. *NO CALLS TO OR FROM MIRANDA!*

Cut off.

Sitting in her father's Volvo, she still felt trapped. The storm had ended, but the morning fog was thick. Traffic was terrible. Her dad wove through the Crescent Bay High parking lot, past the buses crawling through the mist. He didn't

15

stop until he was right next to the flagpole, as if Miranda would skip town if she were dropped off as far back as the loading zone.

Even after her father had stepped on the brake, Miranda sat in the front seat, staring out the windshield . . . waiting for her cell door to be opened.

"I'm only letting you come early to give this speech because I know how much your class means to you," her father said. "I know how hard you and your class worked to raise money for your new quad, and I don't want you to get out of touch."

Miranda stared straight ahead. Everything blurred in front of her, as if her old two-story high school was behind smoky glass.

"Your mother will pick you up right after school again." Her father checked his briefcase, which rested between them on the seat, along with his pin-striped suit jacket and a Great Books audiotape. He sat back, and the automatic locks flicked up.

"Fine," Miranda muttered.

Clutching her briefcase and her disorganized speech written on three-by-five cards, she finally undid her seat belt and reached for the door handle. Her dad leaned over, tapping the sleeve of her blazer. "By the way," he added in a softer voice. "I arranged for you to talk to Eric."

"What?" Miranda panicked.

"Next Tuesday," her father clarified. "I think he deserves an explanation."

Miranda thought she deserved the chance to say, No! I don't want to deal with Eric. Not yet! Maybe not ever. She pictured Eric's strong, single-minded face. The captain of the Crescent Bay High football team, Eric planned his life as if it were a series of football plays. Miranda used to be even worse, as if her life were something that could be charted in an appointment book. But now everything had changed and she could barely organize her activity announcements.

"I think that if you are honest and considerate of Eric's feelings, if you explain and apologize and don't have any more contact with . . . that other boy," her father pronounced, "we can begin to lift this punishment soon."

Miranda stared into the blur of fog again. She tried not to picture Jackson's face. Just thinking about him might give away everything about their meeting the night before. She worked for the old Miranda control.

Miranda finally leaned her shoulder against the car door and stumbled out. She hugged her soft leather briefcase, stepping into a shallow puddle in her riding boots.

She passed the school's old sea lion statue, then squeezed into the overheated hall. Locker doors slammed. Voices echoed. Even though football season was over, Eric's picture as team captain still hung in the trophy case. But football spirit banners had been replaced by posters for girls' volleyball. Miranda turned away from it, breathing in the same smell of meat loaf and green beans that had greeted her every Thursday since freshman year.

Miranda headed for the quad, until two high, excited voices lifted above the noise of the growing crowd.

"MIRANDA!"

"MIRAAAANDAAA! OH, MY GOD. WAIT UP!"

Miranda turned. She caught the soft sheen of Kat's hair, still damp from the storm or that morning's swim practice. She waved to Jojo Hernandez, the third of their grade-school trio, who was right next to Kat, bustling along in an eye-popping yellow rain slicker, five bracelets on one wrist and her brilliant, cheerleader's smile on full. Miranda hadn't spoken to Jojo at all since the formal. She'd barely seen any of their old group, which included Kat and Jojo, Kat's radio partner Gabe, and his best friend, Chip Kohler. And formerly . . . Eric.

Jojo reached Miranda first. She grabbed Miranda's arm, her gold bracelets jangling and her long, painted nails almost digging into Miranda's skin. Each of Jojo's nails was painted a different color and decorated with a letter, spelling out C.R.E.S.C.E.N.T. H.I.

"Finally, I found you! Let's go where we can talk," Jojo cried, pulling Miranda toward a janitors' closet. "I've been so worried about you."

Miranda let herself be dragged in. Kat quickly followed, and the three of them squeezed together, surrounded by crates of paper towels and a mop in a pail. Miranda winced from the soapy smell.

As soon as they were inside, Jojo started, "Miranda! I can't believe this is the first time I've seen you since the formal," she bubbled. "I mean, except for two seconds between classes! What is happening to our crowd? I've missed you so much. How are you? Where have you been at lunch all week? Did you get my phone messages? Why did you leave the formal? What happened with Eric! Are you all right?"

"Answer her in one word," Kat teased.

Miranda took in Kat's sensitive face, then looked back at Jojo's dark, springy curls, wide smile and news-hungry eyes.

"Tell all!" Jojo insisted, bouncing up and down on her aerobic shoes, her bracelets jingling. Her voice had a passionate ring to it, as if she were rousing a cheering crowd. "I've already waited so long to find out all about this. I've missed you so much. I can't stand it."

Miranda put a hand to her face. As happy as she was to see Jojo, she blinked to protect herself from Jojo's five-hundred-watt energy.

"Are you okay, Miranda?" Kat leaned in and whispered.

"I'm okay," Miranda told Kat. "I'm ready to introduce your special KHOT show in my announcements this morning. I hope I do a decent job."

"Don't worry," Jojo chattered. "You're only the best public speaker in our class. And Kat and Gabe don't need much publicity. They'll have a captive audience for tomorrow's show during lunch."

"Gee, thanks, Jojo," Kat laughed.

Jojo beamed, putting her arm around Kat and hugging her. "If it weren't for you and Gabe, I don't know what we'd all do. Our quad is being fixed up, so we can't eat there until the new grass is ready." She popped a piece of bubble gum in her mouth. "The cafeteria is being remodeled, so that's off limits for the next two weeks. If you ask me, our entire lunchtime social life has been destroyed. Do you know, after we worked *so* hard to raise the money to fix up the quad, now they're fixing it up all right, but they've taken away *our* table."

"Really?" Miranda asked. All week Miranda had been hiding out during lunch, eating in her fifth-period chemistry classroom with a few science nerds who didn't even know who she was. And now she would be meeting Jackson off campus during lunch. Since the Turnaround Formal, she hadn't given much thought to their group or their old lunch place.

Kat nodded. "Jojo's telling the truth. Our old lunch table is gone."

"Now all of us have to brown-bag it and eat in the auditorium until the cafeteria is finished." Jojo fished a decorated pink lunch sack out of her book bag and held it up. "The only thing that will save us is that Kat and Gabe are doing a Totally Hot show live tomorrow while we eat. I can't wait."

Kat mugged a show of nerves, pretending to

bite her hand. "It won't really even be a radio show" — she shrugged — "since we won't actually broadcast. It was Gabe's idea."

"Well, it was a great idea," Jojo cheered. "I say so. Everyone says so."

There was a lull in the conversation as Jojo applauded Kat. After that, Jojo looked from Kat to Miranda and back again.

"Well, I'd better go," Miranda finally said, remembering her speech and starting toward the closet door.

Jojo stopped her. "Speaking of what everybody's talking about, Miranda," she said in a more serious tone.

"What?" Miranda asked.

"I'd better warn you." Jojo opened her dark eyes, moved close to Miranda, and whispered. "Okay. Lisa Avery is really trying to stir things up for you. She told Janet Thomas, who told Shelley Lara, who told me that Lisa is furious that you won Princess at the formal and then ran out and didn't even accept it. She says the least you could have done is let the committee know you didn't want to win. I guess Lisa was sure *she* was going to win instead."

"Lisa!" Miranda objected. She and Jojo had been with Kat to see Lisa wrapped around Brent

Tucker at the Turnaround Formal. And that wasn't the first time that Miranda had known Lisa to backstab someone. Earlier that fall Lisa had stuffed the ballot box to try and win homecoming queen. Then, after Lisa still lost for queen, but Miranda won junior princess, Lisa told everyone that the voting had been rigged.

"Don't worry about it too much, Miranda," Jojo backtracked. "People will forget about the Turnaround Formal, Lisa or no Lisa." She glanced at Kat. "Sorry to even mention Lisa's name. I know I used to be friends with her, but she is no longer on my list."

Kat's face had clouded over. She played with the crazy necklace she often wore, a piece of twine from which she hung various oddball belongings. That day it held her swimming goggles and a pin that read, *Back off.*

Miranda made another attempt to go.

"Miranda, I have to find a way to talk to you," Kat suddenly blurted out in a funny, private voice. "Something happened after I got home last night. Is there any way we can get together? I have to meet Gabe at the radio station during lunch today to rehearse, but is there any way your dad would let me talk to you if I call tonight?"

"Wait a minute!" Jojo bristled, looking back and forth betweeen Miranda and Kat. "Back up here. What are you talking about, Kat? Something happened after you got home last night from where?"

Miranda ignored Jojo. "I need to talk to you again, too," she told Kat. "But I still can't get phone calls. My dad even checks my mail, just to make sure I don't get anything from . . ." Miranda glanced at Jojo, then clammed up.

"From who?" Jojo prodded again, her brown eyes opening wider. *"WHO?* What are you two talking about?"

Miranda checked her announcement speech notes, then looked at her watch.

"WHO?" Jojo repeated, glancing at Kat. "WHAT? Miranda, what were you going to say?"

"I'd better get going." Miranda started to ease out of the closet, then turned back to Kat. "Kat, maybe early next week you could tell my dad you need me to tutor you in algebra. I bet he'd let you come over if you said that."

"But I don't take algebra," Jojo pointed out in a sharp voice.

"Jojo, my dad would never let me have both of you over," Miranda mumbled. She couldn't afford the risk of Jojo spreading the word about Jackson. Her father was right about one thing. She owed Eric the courtesy of telling him about Jackson before he heard it through locker-room gossip. "If you came over, too, my dad would know it was purely social."

The sparkle in Jojo's eyes turned hard.

Miranda exchanged glances with Kat. "I really have to go. I have to give my report in a few minutes."

Jojo looked away. "We'll be cheering for you."

"Thanks," Miranda said.

Miranda left them behind, hurrying across the hall and across the quad toward the library, where she was going to give her announcements. There was already a crowd gathered at the library entrance, looking back at the new quad, which was completely roped off. Between last night's rain and that morning's fog, the new grass looked soggy and smelled like a marsh.

Ducking through the crowd and into the library foyer, Miranda quickly looked around for Jackson. He was just inside, near the career research shelf and the college catalogs. He stood with his newspaper cronies, wearing a soft sweater with a long white scarf. Miranda kept going, treasuring a quick glimpse of his curious eyes and warm, crooked smile.

The sophomore class president was finishing his report, so Miranda moved fast to make it to the lectern. She managed the old confident Miranda stride, with her briefcase tucked under her arm, until she passed the final crowd of senior girls. Although the girls were standing only a few feet from the podium, they chattered among themselves as if they were out in the student parking lot. Miranda only needed a glimpse to recognize their leader. Lisa Avery.

With a sausage-tight leather skirt, a fluffy off-the-shoulder sweater, and brassy red hair, Lisa had always reminded Miranda of a Barbie doll. Right now her heavily glossed mouth pouted and puckered, encouraging her followers to comment loudly as Miranda passed by.

"I don't know why everyone ever thought she was so perfect . . ."

"Really. Talk about heartless. Poor Eric. . . ."

"I don't care how good her grades are and how much she's done for the school. Miranda Jamison is just selfish."

Feeling like she wanted to hide under the reference books, Miranda then heard Mr. Shorestein, the junior class adviser, making her introduction.

"And here's the girl who always promotes her class spirit and puts in endless hours of hard work. One of our strongest leaders at Crescent Bay High, Miranda Jamison."

Miranda stepped up to the lectern, and polite applause began.

"Let me see." Miranda began in an unsure voice. "Junior activities for the next two weeks." She cleared her throat. "Tomorrow Kat McDonough and Gabe Sachs will entertain the upperclass during lunch with a live version of Totally Hot, their famous radio show. Friends in Need, our peer counseling program, will have another workshop for new student counselors. . . ."

Miranda continued to read from her three-by-five cards, even though her voice was shaky. As hard as she tried to concentrate, she kept hearing the nasty gossip and seeing her father's disappointed face. For the first time, she had begun to wonder if her leap into freedom and love had really been worth it.

THREE

"What's for lunch?" Gabe asked Kat that day at noon.

Kat sighed and sorted through the goodies she'd brought in her little brother's Ninja Turtles lunch box. "My mom's homemade muffins. Soup. Apple slices. And a Swiss cheese sandwich."

"That's what I like about you," Gabe teased, nudging her and taking half her sandwich. "You're always so homey and domestic."

"Yeah, right," Kat said. "Get it yourself, Mac."

Gabe took a bite and smiled. "Mm. And she can cook, too."

They were sitting in the hall outside the radio station, quickly stuffing their mouths before going in to rehearse — since Gabe got finicky about getting crumbs in the radio console. Kat didn't mind stalling for a few minutes. Actually, she was grateful to just sit with Gabe and joke the way they used to. With Gabe she never used to worry about holding back or going out of control. They were just buddies. Plain, simple and calm. But since Brent Tucker had entered her life, even things between her and Gabe had gotten strained.

But Gabe looked anything but strained as he devoured half of Kat's sandwich, then sorted through the other bags and tinfoil packages her mom had packed inside the lunch box. His dark hair fell in its usual easy curls. His muscular body looked relaxed in his classic worn black jeans and black one-pocket T-shirt — his lack of money turned to personal fashion statement. His DJ voice sounded resonant and bouncy as he hummed some old rock song.

Kat opened the thermos of soup and offered him a spoonful. "You know, Gabe, I think you like not being able to eat in the cafeteria. Everybody has to bring food from home, so you don't have to borrow money for lunch. You just mooch."

Gabe took another slurp of soup. "That's me. Gabe the moocher. Hey, since I don't have to borrow money today, how about if I borrow your World Civ book for fifth period?"

Kat reached in her book sack, her old sewing class gym bag to which she added plastic dinosaurs, weird buttons, and a special joke pocket, where she kept a little notepad in case a good joke came to her when she was in the hall or on her way to swim practice. She handed the textbook to Gabe.

"Thanks," he said, flipping through it.

Kat leaned over him and plucked out her assignment. "You can't borrow my homework, though. And get this book back to me before school tomorrow."

"I won't forget." He stood up and wiped his hands on his jeans. "I'm not the forgetful one these days."

"What do you mean?" she asked, standing up, too, and closing the thermos.

"This morning before school," Gabe reminded. "You were supposed to help me move the audio equipment over to the auditorium for our live show tomorrow. Remember?"

Kat stared blankly for a moment. "Oh, my God!" she suddenly recalled. "That's right. I'm sorry." Between all the craziness with Brent and Miranda, she had completely forgotten. "Jojo and I ran into Miranda this morning and then I went to hear her give the announcements in the library. I guess I got preoccupied."

"I guess so." Gabe stared at her. "It's okay," he decided. "Chip helped me instead."

"Good old Chip."

"Yeah. Good old Chip." Gabe opened the door to the radio station hallway, then turned back to her. "Just do me a favor, though, and don't forget anything else while we're doing our show tomorrow."

"I won't. Gabe, come on. Have I ever dried up when we were on the air?"

Gabe shrugged and swung his army surplus pack over his shoulder.

"Don't answer that," Kat said, suddenly remembering her first meeting with Brent. That had been during a KHOT radio show, after he'd first arrived at Crescent Bay High and came for an interview. It had been a classic brain-in-the-wastebasket moment for Kat. Face-to-face with gorgeous Brent, Kat had not only dried up, she'd left a hole in the airwaves as big as the Grand Canyon.

No longer able to meet Gabe's green eyes, Kat tossed him the last hunk of muffin, then gave him a push into the hall.

"Hey, I have this new idea for tomorrow's live show," Gabe explained as they walked down the dusty hallway that went through the audiovisual room and into the tiny radio station.

"Oh, yeah? What's your new idea?"

Gabe spun and walked backwards. "How about putting an extra microphone down on the auditorium floor and starting the show with questions from the audience?"

"Questions from the audience?" Kat stopped at the door to the station, which was open a crack. She waited before barging in, just in case she might interrupt a radio drama rehearsal or some person from the electronics club. "What do you mean?"

"We introduce some of our better known radio characters." Gabe gestured excitedly. "The ones that everybody knows well from previous shows, like the Lounge Lizard and Patty Prom Queen. People ask our characters questions, and we make up funny answers on the spot. I think it's a good idea. We're both so fast on our feet. I think it'll work."

Kat was considering the idea, but when she opened the door to the radio station, she was too stunned to even remember what Gabe had just said. Someone had filled the radio station with flowers. Long-stemmed fresh flowers had been strewn everywhere, as if it were the back room of a florist's shop.

Gabe stepped in, too, took in the flowers, and started to laugh. "All right," he grinned. "Now this is the kind of greeting we deserve. I guess someone likes our show."

"Who did this?" Kat cried, as she looked around with her eyes popping out. Roses covered the console. Daisies littered the CD racks. Pink mums were scattered all over the floor. The smell was so overpowering that it almost made her lose her balance. "Maybe it's something left over from a drama project."

"Maybe somebody croaked," Gabe joked as he came in and looked around. He scooped up a long-stemmed red rose, sniffed it, and stuck it through his belt loop. "More likely, some poor girl took my flirting a little too seriously," he boasted. "I've had female admirers before, but no girl ever went this far."

That was when Kat noticed the note taped to the back of her chair. When she saw the name written on the envelope, her thoughts became a jumble and her legs felt weak.

"Gabe," she said.

He was still smiling and smelling the roses. "Hm?"

"I hate to tell you."

"What?"

"The flowers aren't for you."

"They're not?"

"They're for me."

Kat opened the envelope, as frightened as if she were opening a letter bomb. She slowly pulled out the pale blue paper and read the neat script.

> *Kat. I figured this would be the best place to leave these for you, and if you didn't find them first, then I would consider it a gift to my new school.*
>
> *I'm not going away. I'll be there for you. Or I'll be there for your friends. I will announce something over the PA or graffiti your name on the gym. I promise you, I'll find a way to prove to you that I am the one. I don't give up.*
> *Brent.*

Kat was so overwhelmed that she didn't know what to do. Brent's words blurred before her eyes. She couldn't think. She couldn't respond. She could barely breathe.

Gabe crept up and looked over her shoulder. After reading the note, he slammed a fist against the console, then turned away. "What did he do?" he barked. "Rob a flower store?"

Kat wanted to laugh the flowers off. She wanted to joke and put a rose between her teeth and go on with their rehearsal. But she wasn't able to do anything but look at the flowers, re-read the note, and feel overwhelmed at what it all could possibly mean. "Gabe. I'm sorry," she finally mumbled. "I can't rehearse right now. I need to take a break and figure this out."

"Great!" Gabe swore, plucking the rose out of his belt loop and flinging it on the floor. Then he leaned over and swept the flowers off the console with such violence that a few bounced off the wall.

Kat clutched her gym bag and lunch box. She tripped over the flowers, lurching to the door-way. She stopped and tried to catch her breath. For a moment she couldn't remember where she was or what she was going to do next.

As she stumbled down the hall, she heard Gabe yell after her, "GREAT REHEARSAL, KAT. SEE YOU TOMORROW IN THE AU-

DITORIUM. THAT IS, IF YOU STILL CARE
ABOUT DOING OUR SHOW!"

"Chip, will you hold this for me?"

"Sure, Jojo."

"Thanks. This, too?"

"Okaaaay."

"Sorry I'm so disorganized, but without our
regular lunch place, nothing feels right. I know.
With Miranda and Eric broken up and Kat and
Gabe rehearsing for their show, maybe we don't
need a lunch place today. But what about after
today? I guess I just worry that our group could
fall apart."

"Jojo, we won't fall apart. People are just
going through some changes."

"Oh, Chip. Don't give me that people-
change, everything-has-its-season routine. I'm
serious."

"I know, Jo."

By the time lunchtime was almost over, an
avalanche of loneliness had landed on Jojo. If Jojo
had to sum up her entire life in one word, that
word would be — FRIENDS. But only that
morning, Miranda — one of her closest, oldest
friends — had needed help. And instead of turn-

ing to Jojo, Miranda had excluded her. Not only
that, but Kat seemed to have some kind of secret,
too, which she hadn't wanted to share. Add to
that the loss of her crowd's lunch place, and Jojo
was feeling thoroughly left out.

Working to throw off her gloom, Jojo
searched through her locker, loading Chip up
with her pompoms, hair dryer, old valentines,
address book, French manual, calorie counter,
and makeup mirror. At least Chip could always
be counted on, with his soft features and
shoulder-length hair, his baggy clothes and laid-
back sixties attitude.

"Jojo," Chip said. He tried to flick his long,
blond hair out of his eyes, but couldn't move
easily under all of Jojo's stuff. "Did you find
what you were looking for? Not that I mind
helping you, but I wanted to get to my environ-
mental studies class early today."

Jojo scrambled through the notes and papers
piled on her locker floor. She had to find the one
thing she knew would cheer her up — a list of
friends she was always revising and looking
over. Jojo was meticulous about doing everything possible to always act nice and keep her
friends friendly.

"Got it," Jojo announced with great relief. She tugged a folded paper out from under her French book.

"Good," Chip breathed, starting to hand things back.

Jojo held up her hand. "Wait, wait, wait . . ." She opened the paper, which had been folded and unfolded so many times before it almost fell apart in her hands. It was a long list, divided into sections and arranged in order of importance. She'd always told herself that without all those names, she might as well be weirdo loner Leanne Heard, who had the locker next to hers.

But since the Turnaround Formal, something new had occurred to Jojo. She'd suddenly started wondering if she had become too obsessed with friends. She had the sense deep down that Miranda and Kat were both dealing with something beyond friendship. She'd had that same feeling last summer after Kat had fallen for that out-of-town guy. Suddenly Kat and Miranda had private codes and secret looks, as if anything having to do with passion was too much for smiley, airhead, nicey nice Jojo to understand.

"What's that list?" Chip asked. "What are you doing? Planning a party?"

Jojo barely paid attention to him. Chip was

one of those friends who wasn't very exciting, but was always dependable and nice. Maybe she was like that, too. Maybe that's why she was not only excluded from conversations about love and sex, but she'd never experienced those things herself. Finally she began to remove belongings from his arms and put them back into her locker.

Chip relaxed his arms. "You know, Jo, nobody's had a really good party for a while."

Jojo shook her head, knowing that Chip rarely had anything important to say, unless what you were passionate about was rare owls or reusing trash. A party was fine, if you had someone to share it with or someone to meet. And yet, even as she crammed her last few things in and made Chip help her close the door, his words began to echo in her head.

PARTY.

Maybe that wasn't such a bad idea. Surprises happened at parties, even if you were the hostess. There was certainly more of a chance of something intriguing happening at a party than over onion rings at their usual weekend hangout, the Wave Cafe.

Chip was already headed down the hall. Jojo took a running stag leap past Leanne's locker to catch up to him.

"CHIP!" she cried, tugging on his backpack and almost making him trip. She turned him around and grinned into his sweet, fine-featured face. "YES."

"Yes, what?"

"Yes, I'm having a party, Chip," she announced, feeling more energetic with each passing second. "For once this year you have had a brilliant idea."

He gave her a mild smile but kept walking backward toward his class. "Gee, thanks."

"Chip, did you hear me?" Jojo demanded, jumping into his path. "I'm going to take you up on your idea. Do you have plans for two weeks from this Saturday?"

"I'll check my calendar," Chip joked.

"Of course you're free." She grinned. "Because that's when I'm going to throw my party. *Our* party, since it was your idea. It'll be at my house, but you're going to help! I'm so glad I talked this over with you. You had such a good idea!"

Chip nodded in his good-natured way. "Whatever you say, Jojo."

FOUR

Kat and Gabe had been let out of fourth period a few minutes early to get ready for their live KHOT show. Standing on the edge of the auditorium stage, Kat was staring into a cracked mirror left over from the fall musical. She took in her blonde hair, walking shorts, suspenders, and desert boots. She clutched her twine necklace. That morning she'd attached a water pistol, a dried flower, a question mark, and the rabbit's foot Miranda had given her in sixth grade — Kat wasn't sure whether she needed luck for herself or for Miranda.

"You ready for this show?" Gabe asked in a curt voice. He was behind the table they'd set up in the middle of the stage the morning before. His sunglasses were resting on his nose. Snapping his fingers to a tune in his head, he checked the microphone.

Kat tucked her T-shirt in and pulled up her socks. "I'm ready. I'm always ready," she mumbled. "That's me. Ready or not, here I go."

"It would have been better if we'd rehearsed yesterday," Gabe said coolly. "I looked for you after school. Where were you? Did you run after Tucker so you could thank him for the flowers?"

"It's none of your business," Kat said.

"Isn't it?"

Kat started across the stage. "I'm having a hard enough time making up my mind about Brent."

"Are you? Well, I can tell you what I think."

"Gabe, I don't really care what you think."

"Any guy who sends a girl that many flowers is trying to cover up something."

"Gabe!" Suddenly something inside Kat went crazy. She lunged over the table and slugged him, swiping at him with the side of her arm. "You don't know anything about Brent!" she exploded. "Would you please stop talking about him!"

Gabe caught her and held on. For a moment they stared into each other's eyes with anger and something else that Kat didn't understand.

Gabe finally let her go and went back to testing the sound effects box.

Kat sat down in front of her microphone. She *had* gone to look for Brent after school the day before, but she hadn't found him. She'd looked for Miranda, too, but she hadn't found her, either. She'd only found Jojo babbling about the great party she'd decided to give. Jojo had gone on and on about how she was going to get their little crowd back together, while inviting everyone else that mattered, too. And then Jojo had chattered about intentionally excluding Lisa Avery, as if the mere fact that Lisa would be left out of her party would solve all of Kat's wildly confusing feelings over Brent and what had happened at the Turnaround Formal.

Just as Gabe flipped a toggle switch on the sound effects box, projecting a duck quack followed by the splat of a breaking egg, he was interrupted by the scream of the real Crescent Bay High bell. The rumble exploding out in the hall reminded Kat of a stampede. Junior/senior lunch had begun.

"Here we go," Kat gasped, grabbing Gabe's shoulder without realizing she'd done it.

Gabe froze. He stared at her hand.

When Gabe finally looked away again, Kat clenched the table edge instead. Then she stared at the crowd as upperclassmen began to pour into the auditorium and holler up at her.

"All right, KHOT!"

"Hi, Kat."

"Gaaaabe," squealed a group of admiring girls.

Gabe flirted back at the girls, and Kat forced a happy mask onto her face. She mugged at friends, and tried to think of jokes for the opening of the show. Meanwhile, she looked out for Miranda, and for Jackson, too. And she looked for Brent, of course. But she didn't find any of them.

"Hey, Kat."

Kat nodded to football captain Eric, Miranda's ex. Hunky and slow in his letter jacket and cowboy boots, he offered a sad wave, then took a seat in the far corner. Next, Jojo came right up to the edge of the stage with Chip.

"KHOT FOREVER!" Jojo cheered, doing a little leap in her red-and-white cheerleader outfit. She tried to communicate some piece of gossip that Kat couldn't hear over what was now a deafening racket.

At the same time Chip stuck two fingers up in a peace symbol, then put them behind Jojo's head. Jojo swatted him.

Gabe poised his hand over the tonearm, getting ready for the opening of the show. The theme music to *Gilligan's Island* began, and Kat whispered to herself, "Let's run with it, partner." Then she and Gabe began humming into kazoos.

"Hello, Crescent Bay High Sea Lions," Kat said, her voice ringing out over the crowd's chatter. "It's a totally new Totally Hot today, coming to you live and in person and in the flesh."

Gabe did a few sea lion barks, which turned into howls and were repeated by some seniors in the front row.

Right away, Kat launched into her first character, Miss Grundy, her prim society-lady character. "Hello boys and girls."

"HELLLLLO!" the upperclassmen responded in corny unison.

"As you all know," Kat pronounced primly, "our overcrowded campus is getting a face-lift, which is why we're all dining in the dear old auditorium."

Gabe cut in. "And in honor of our radical new quad and unfinished cafeteria, we're doing something radical here on Totally Hot today. We are giving you the chance to talk to your favorite KHOT characters, to ask those questions you've always wanted to ask of Miss Grundy . . ."

Kat bunched up her face again and gestured to the second mike they'd set up on the auditorium floor.

Gabe slid his sunglasses down his nose. "Also available upon request will be Mitch Make-It-Up, dumb jock of I Don't Know High; Willa Bradford, smoking patrol meter maid, and your favorites, Larry Lounge Lizard and that southern belle whose dance card is always full, Patty Prom Queen. Ask us anything." Gabe winked at the girls in the front row.

"Well, *almost* anything," Kat corrected.

About six people seemed to stand at the same time, their seats snapping up as they raced to the front of the room.

When Lisa Avery slithered in front of the others, Kat's whole body went on red-hot alert. She stared down at Lisa's flaming auburn hair, which was pulled back with a glittery comb on one side, while the other side waved over one eye. In spandex pants and a boat-necked sweater that sagged to expose her shoulders, Lisa stepped up to the microphone.

"I'd like to ask the first question," Lisa said, her voice so breathy that it sounded like an amplified wind storm.

"Ask away, Lisa," Gabe flirted. "I wouldn't mind asking you a few questions myself."

The crowd laughed.

Lisa flipped back her hair, then touched the corner of her gooey mouth. "I wanted to ask the society lady an etiquette question about her best friend Miranda Jamison."

"What?" Kat managed as gasps and whispers flew around the room.

Lisa licked her lips. "Miss Grundy, since you are the Miss Manners of Crescent Bay High, I wanted to know what you thought of the way Miranda ditched her boyfriend at the Turnaround Formal."

Static filled Kat's brain and she couldn't think of a response. All Kat could think was that for the second time in one semester she'd wanted to wring Lisa's sexy, white neck.

After waiting for Kat, Gabe leaned into the mike to fill the dead air. "I like good manners," he said as dumb jock Mitch. "Please. Thank you. And all that junk." The crowd laughed, then Gabe elbowed Kat.

While Kat still struggled to think of a reply, Lisa said, "That's all. I just wanted to know what you thought." Then she fell back into a guy's lap, kicking her shapely legs and wiggling.

"Miss Grundy, do you have a response?" Gabe prompted angrily.

Kat's mind was still a confused, furious blank.

Gabe grabbed at the sound effects box, randomly flipping switches, trying to get the crowd's attention again, but the whispers and gasps were filling the place like a flood. Finally someone else stepped up to the audience mike, knocking it with his palm and sending out a scream of feedback.

"Hello," the boy at the mike said tentatively. "May I say something?"

It was Brent, with his golden hair flopping over his forehead and his blue eyes downcast. He had his hands in the pockets of his uncreased khakis, which he wore with a turtleneck and argyle vest. Kat's heart started thumping so loudly she thought her microphone would pick it up.

"Can everybody quiet down for one second?" Brent demanded. Even his voice was elegant and sure. "I think it's great that KHOT came here to entertain us today, and I think we can at least give them our attention."

The infectious chatter slowly turned to shrugs

and nods. Gabe leaned forward to take over again, but Brent beat him to it.

"Anyway, I'd like to talk to Patty Prom Queen," Brent projected in a careful voice. "I don't know about manners, but I'd like to ask Patty what she thinks about the way people act at dances and proms."

"Well, I'm certainly an expert on that," Kat managed. Gabe was staring at her and narrowing his eyes.

Brent flicked back his hair. "I wanted to answer Lisa, too, I guess. Just because someone does something thoughtless at *one* formal dance, that's no reason to write that person off."

Lisa suddenly stood back up, her shiny mouth pursed in fury.

"I just wanted to ask Patty," Brent added, "if she doesn't think that people make mistakes and deserve a second chance."

Nearly numb, Kat finally pulled back to take in the crowd again. Lisa looked furious. The outraged whispers were being replaced by thoughtful nods. In that moment Kat knew that Brent had taken the first step toward getting Miranda back into the swing of things.

"Patty," she suddenly heard Gabe prompt in

a very tense voice, *"what do you have to say in response?"*

Kat knew that she'd let Brent get in the way of the show again, and that Gabe was furious with her. She tried to remember all the funny things she'd planned to say, but her brain was turning into mush again. Finally, she smiled down at Brent and said in her own breathless voice, "All right, Brent. I'll give that some thought."

"That's all I ask," Brent said over the mike. He stuck his hands in his pockets and smiled, his eyes glued to Kat.

"Thank you, Patty Prom Queen," Gabe barked. "Even though you no longer have a southern accent, we are all interested in your comments."

As Gabe began reading off upcoming events and plugging the girls' volleyball team, Kat still sat there, silent as a post. She stared down at Brent while he smiled up at her. Meanwhile, Gabe kept glancing back and forth between them as his famous DJ voice grew tighter and more tense.

While most of the upperclass was in the auditorium listening to the radio show, Jackson was still stuck in the journalism room.

He'd had to proof two articles for the upcoming issue of *Bay News*, plus decide whether to put the story about girls' volleyball in the sports section or on the front page. In addition, he'd been trying to finish a story of his own about the Friends in Need peer counseling program. And most important of all, he'd been trying to get off campus to meet the girl he'd been thinking about all day, even all week.

Miranda.

Miranda, Miranda . . . He'd been wanting to yell it out loud since the fourth-period bell. His staffers would come up to him wanting to know about this photo and that deadline, and he'd only wanted to blurt out one thing.

Not now! I'm on my way to meet Miranda!

But of course he couldn't say that, and it was driving him crazy. He couldn't think of anything to say but, sorry . . . excuse me . . . um, well, gotta go . . .

By the middle of lunch he was almost ready to spill everything. Miranda was waiting for him again at the vacant lot across the street, and if he didn't get going he'd miss her completely. It was Friday. If he didn't see her now, he wouldn't be able to see her again until after the weekend.

But when he grabbed his leather jacket and headed for the door, the other reporters and *Bay News* staffers followed, blocking his path, all of them talking at once.

"I know this story is dull, Jackson, but I'm not sure how to spice it up."

"Jackson, can you show me how to cut and paste again on the computer? I forgot."

"Jackson, remember that radical story you wrote about Mr. Potato Head? Can I get a copy of that?"

Jackson finally threw up his hands. "ENOUGH!" he exploded in an exasperated and uncharacteristic tone.

His staff looked shocked for a moment, then Jackson forced a laugh. "I'm sorry. I have to go. I'll try and be back before lunch is over. I have a . . . dentist appointment."

"Oh," his staffers responded, looking relieved and a little confused.

Sarah Donovan, the paper's photographer, pointed a finger at him. "Okay, Jackson, but remember that we have a deadline. We have a paper to put out!"

Jackson hesitated, seeing the suspicion in Sarah's eyes. Then he was out the door, leaving the computers, the headlines, and the drafting tables to his staff. He stopped briefly at his locker to pick up his skateboard, then hurried past the activity bulletin board and through the student parking lot. Double-checking to see that nobody was watching, he put the skateboard down.

Glide.

In a second he was on Holiday Street, so excited he didn't notice he was heading right into traffic. He kept pace though, leaned and pushed off, glided and rolled until he caught a glimpse of Miranda waiting for him on the edge of the vacant lot.

She waved.

Thoughts of *Bay News* flew out of Jackson's head as he coasted and swerved, long legs bent, spiky dark hair ruffling in the breeze. His leather jacket flapped behind him as he mouthed thanks to a car for stopping midblock, tapping the hood as he passed.

When he reached the lot, he leaped onto the sidewalk, momentarily leaving his skateboard in the gutter. He ran to her. They came together, and he twirled her around in his arms, buried his face against her neck. Then he put his hand in the back of her long hair, and they kissed hard, until they both stumbled onto the rough sand.

"I'm sorry I'm late," Jackson gasped, scrambling to his feet again and trying to catch his breath. He fetched his skateboard, then swung his backpack off his shoulder. They raced to the back corner of the sandy lot where they tumbled down again, legs entwined, bodies close. "I couldn't get away from everybody after class today," Jackson explained. Pretending that he was about to pass out, he flopped his forehead on Miranda's shoulder. "I didn't know how to tell Sarah why I had to go. I'm not used to avoiding the people I work with. It was weird."

Miranda grabbed the lapels of his leather jacket and pressed her forehead against his chin. "It's even weirder for me not to have tons of people asking me things. I can't stand it. It's like overnight I've become invisible."

"You sure don't look invisible to me." Jackson ran his hand down the side of her face, then finally sat with his arms around his knees.

She sat next to him with a sad smile as the breeze blew hair across her mouth. "At least I get to see Kat again next week. My dad's letting her come over."

"And Eric," Jackson reminded her.

Miranda took a deep breath. "And Eric."

"What are you going to tell him?"

Miranda shook her head, then sifted some sand through her fist.

"Tell him everything," Jackson insisted. "Just tell him the truth." The truth. Even as Jackson's words floated into the breeze, he thought about how hard that might be. Still, Jackson had never believed in taking the easy way out. "You have to talk to him sometime. We can't keep this up forever."

"I know. I've been thinking about that all week."

"Do you know what I've thought about all week?"

Miranda shook her head.

Jackson tossed a few stones onto the middle of the lot, then looked up at the sky. "I thought about how I've always wanted to shake things up. I've always believed in facing what's out there, letting it explode, and then picking up the pieces."

Miranda looked right at him, her eyes betraying a little fear. "And now?"

"Now the only thing that's shaken up is me."

FIVE

"Gabe, what do you think makes girls respect you?"

"Oh Chip, let's not talk about girls. This is Friday night. We're at the Wave Cafe. I'd like to relax."

"Okay, Gabe," Chip persisted. "Not just girls, then. People. Humans. Why do some humans get walked on all the time, while others get away with anything?"

Gabe sensed that Chip was on one of his what-does-it-all-mean, let's talk Zen, soul-searches. Meanwhile, Gabe was trying to enjoy the favorite Crescent Bay High hangout, the Wave Cafe. The jukebox blinked and blasted. Crescent Bay High couples bounced to the vintage tunes. The old statue of King Neptune had been loaded down with empty glasses, and the fish netting hanging from the walls was littered with prom tickets and pictures.

This was the end of a long, frustrating week for Gabe, and all he wanted to do now was relax the knot that had formed deep inside his chest. The knot had started last Saturday when he'd had to watch Kat and Brent at the Turnaround Formal. It had gotten even tighter when Brent had dumped what must have been hundreds of dollars' worth of flowers in his radio station. Add to that the afternoon's live radio show, and Gabe needed more than just to relax. He needed to blow off steam.

Gabe snapped his fingers. "Listen, Chip. If you don't want people to walk all over you, you've just got to draw a line," he advised, thinking about Kat and Brent again. "When somebody is doing something that drives you too crazy, you have to say, 'This is how far I go. No further.' It's that simple."

"It's not simple, man," Chip said, popping a piece of ice into his mouth. "Life is never simple."

Gabe picked up his knife again and rapped a drumbeat on his plate. He didn't want to believe Chip. Gabe wanted life to be simple. He wanted to find a simple antidote for the way he'd been feeling lately and the big knot getting tighter and tighter inside his chest.

Gabe had decided long before he'd teamed up with Kat that there were going to be two kinds of relationships with members of the opposite sex. There would be girls to flirt with and back away from when things got heavy, and there would be friends, who he would never need to flirt with or back away from because things would never ever get heavy.

Kat had always been in the definite friend category. But when he and Kat had rehearsed together in her bedroom one day, Gabe's insides had started taking things seriously. His head had become light. He'd had this overwhelming desire to wrap his arms tight around Kat, to never let her go. Gabe had wanted to touch her hair, to say crazy, heavy things, and kiss her mouth over and over again.

Those feelings were definitely not simple, so Gabe was doing his best to shove them away. He glanced at the next table, where four girls from the Crescent Bay High volleyball team were gathered after that night's game. He and Chip had just come from the game. The girls had won an impressive victory over Gearheart

High. Gabe picked up a Wave napkin and scribbled on it.

> *Volleyball Net-ettes. Amazing game.*
> *You made the shots. Now I am at your*
> *serve-ice. Gabe.*

Before Gabe could wad the message up and bat it in the air, Chip leaned over to read it.

"You are amazing with girls," Chip marveled, pushing his hair out of his eyes to peer back at the volleyball girls. "If I had a thing for one of those volleyball girls, I'd just go over with my mouth hanging open, say 'excuse me' about twelve times and 'great game' about twenty times, and then I'd walk away feeling like a fool."

"There's one big difference," Gabe responded with a grin, pitching his message over to their table. "I don't have a thing for anyone."

Chip shrugged.

While waiting for the volleyball girls to respond to his note, Gabe looked back at Chip. "You don't have a thing for anyone right now, do you? You're not still hung up on Lisa Avery, are you?"

"No way." Chip shook his head. "Not after what she did to Miranda at your show today."

The knot in Gabe's chest tightened again at the mention of that day's show. "I don't know what you saw in Lisa in the first place," Gabe told him. Chip always seemed to be pining over some girl who was too unavailable, too popular, or too weird. "I mean, I know what you *saw* in her, but girls like that are just out to make you miserable."

"Maybe I *let* girls make me miserable," Chip considered.

Before Gabe could respond, an answer to his note bounced off the rim of his water glass, landing right in front of him. The return message was written on a volleyball program in an A-for-penmanship hand.

> *Hi. I'm glad you saw our game. We won! (Gee, I guess you already know that.) By the way, this is from Amy Zandarski. (Me.)*

Knowing that misery was not what he pined for, Gabe patted Chip's shoulder, located Amy, then went over to the volleyball girls. The minute he looked into Amy's innocent brown eyes, he was in his element. Her eager smile was a place where he could coast on the easy wave of a good time, not worry about complications, and always find a simple exit.

"Hi," said Amy, a freckled-faced junior with straight brown hair. Her pink overalls, floral print blouse, and short, bitten fingernails all reminded Gabe of a little kid. It was amazing that such a demure girl could also be such a powerhouse on the volleyball court.

Gabe dropped onto Amy's lap and watched a fierce blush cover her round face. "I watched you on the court tonight," he joked. "Do you play that hard all the time?"

"I guess." Amy giggled so hard she almost couldn't respond. "We practice on the beach every Saturday. You can come and watch anytime."

Gabe knew it was an out-and-out invitation, and he didn't want to make a commitment. So he bounded up again, just offering a wink and shrug. That was also when he noticed Kat and Jojo finally making their way through the crowd like a walking spirit duo. Kat was in a red jumpsuit, and Jojo wore her cheerleader outfit. They'd been at the game, too. It had sure taken a long time for them to make it over to the Wave.

Gabe tousled Amy's hair, then scooted back over to his own table, just as Kat and Jojo were sitting down on either side of Chip.

"I thought for sure we'd see him when we stopped by his parents' resort just now," Jojo was telling Kat. "Of course, I also thought he'd show up at the game tonight. Everybody else was there. Except Miranda, of course."

"I just wanted to thank him for what he said at the show today," Kat said, smiling.

"And for the flowers," Jojo giggled. "I'm so glad you finally told me what was going on. Boy, was I wrong about him!"

They were talking about Brent, Gabe realized, as the knot in his chest grabbed at him again.

Jojo redid her lipstick, then stood right up again. "Okay. I need to make the rounds right away," she announced, patting her tight, dark curls. "I put party invitations in peoples' lockers first thing this morning, and I have to make sure that everyone got them."

"Everyone?" Kat whispered, pointing to Lisa Avery, who was leaning over a table near the front door, chatting with her usual crowd of flirty senior girls.

Chip turned, then let his hair cover his face.

"And I have to avoid the people I didn't invite.

Or rather, the one person I didn't invite." Jojo tugged Chip's sleeve. "Chip, come with me. I may need a distraction if Lisa makes a scene."

Chip gave Gabe a long look, then finally stood up. "I guess I can be a distraction."

Jojo dragged Chip into the brightness and the noise, leaving Kat alone with Gabe.

Gabe stared at Kat, who was bouncing along with the music and smiling as if she'd just won the lottery. For some bizarre reason, he couldn't think of anything to say. All he felt was that dark, tight knot of anger again.

Meanwhile, Kat was still bubbly, snapping her fingers, and humming along with the tunes. The giddier she seemed, the more it drove him crazy. After another few minutes, she finally leaned over and grabbed an onion off his plate. Then she added a dash of ketchup and two olives, borrowed a few curly fries, and made a sculpture in the middle of the table.

Gabe knew that she was trying to joke things up. Before this whole mess with Brent, he would have added to her creation — heck, he would have scooped up food from every plate in the café. Instead, he just stared.

Kat speared a pickle. But instead of using it for her sculpture, she tossed it at him. It landed, *flap*, like a dead eel on his shoulder.

"Sorry," she giggled.

Trying to keep control, Gabe removed the pickle, threw it back onto Chip's plate, and dabbed his T-shirt with a napkin.

"Excuse me. I didn't mean to ruin your favorite shirt," Kat teased.

So Gabe always wore the same five T-shirts and three pairs of jeans. He barely had money for that. The trailer park he lived in with his sister and mother was a far cry from the Tucker Resort. "You want a guy with fancy clothes," he said coolly, "stick with Tucker."

Kat dropped her smile and shook her head. "Gabe, I was just trying to be funny. Can't we forget about Brent for two seconds? Can't we just joke and goof around the way we used to?"

"Sure." He tossed his napkin over her food sculpture. "I'd like that. I'd really like it if you could be funny on our show again, like you used to be."

"What's that supposed to mean?"

Gabe looked right at her. "Just that you turned into Miss Awestruck and Silent again on our show today." He shrugged. "Look, Kat, I don't care what's going on with you and Tucker —

except when it affects our show."

For a moment Kat seemed flustered. "Fine. If this is really about our show, then let's talk about Totally Hot."

Gabe nodded and folded his arms across his chest. "Okay. Let's talk about it."

"Okay. Let's talk about the fact that you and I haven't rehearsed in almost three weeks," Kat pointed out.

"That's not my fault," Gabe objected, remembering that mind-blowing rehearsal in her bedroom again. "You're the one who walked out yesterday!"

"Well, let's rehearse tomorrow then," she sputtered.

"And I can't rehearse tomorrow," he decided. "Amy Zandarski just begged me to watch the volleyball team practice down on the beach. Next Saturday, too."

"Begged. She *begged* you?"

Gabe smirked.

"Begged, Gabe?" Kat repeated, starting to sound angry. "Is that how you think girls should relate to you, Gabe? Do they need to beg?"

"Some do." He offered a macho shrug. "I can't help it."

"Gabe, are you telling me that I should beg you to come over just so we can rehearse our next show again?"

He forced a smile. "You begged Brent to go to the Turnaround dance with you."

Kat shot to her feet. "Would you stop talking about Brent?"

"I'm not talking about him," Gabe insisted, standing up, too. "I'm talking about our show."

"Let's really talk about it then," Kat ranted. "Would you like to know the reason that I'm not always funny anymore?"

"What."

"It has nothing to do with Brent. It has to do with you!" Kat accused, her voice quavering as she yelled over the music.

"Me?"

"YOU!" Kat cried. "You give me these looks on the show, like I should be kicked out of school for allowing two seconds of dead airtime. And then you don't even want to rehearse."

"*You're* the one who doesn't want to rehearse."

"I am not! You're the one who thinks I'm not funny! I don't even know why you want to do the show with me anymore."

"Maybe I don't!"

Kat's mouth fell open. "Well . . . well, maybe I don't either."

"THEN WHY ARE WE DOING THE STU-PID SHOW??!!!" Gabe exploded.

"I DON'T KNOW!"

"SO LET'S NOT DO IT THEN! LET'S JUST FORGET THE DUMB SHOW! FOR GOOD!"

At that moment the jukebox shut off. Kat moved first. Scowling at him, she kicked her chair aside, then stormed over to join Jojo and Chip.

Gabe sat back down as his whole body began to shake. He felt that knot in his chest again, and he thought about the line he'd talked about with Chip. He was right. If he was going to keep things simple, he couldn't let anyone push him too far. Too many lines had already been crossed between him and Kat.

SIX

*T*hunk, *thunk, thunk . . . whapppp.*

At the end of school the following Wednesday, Leanne Heard took in the sound of locker doors slamming and opening, slamming and opening as she made her way down the central hall. An outsider who slunk around in moccasins and a second-hand dress, her hair dyed platinum blonde and her mouth stained crushed-berry red, Leanne prided herself in keeping her distance and making unique observations.

Leanne thought of her classmates leaving their campus as one giant rock song. The lockers slamming were the music. And the lyrics were the chatter Leanne tuned in as she wove through the crowd. Eavesdropping on one of the most popular cliques — Lisa Avery and her senior girl groupies — Leanne decided that today's selection was definitely acid-tongued rock.

"Lisa, I can't believe Jojo really didn't invite you to her party!"

"Well, believe it," Lisa snapped, yanking her sparkly sweater further down her bare shoulder. "Who cares? Jojo's crowd isn't even a crowd anymore. Maybe everyone else has forgotten how Miranda insulted the whole school, but I haven't. And I just heard that Kat McDonough and Gabe Sachs aren't even going to keep doing their radio show anymore."

"Well, everybody's talking about Jojo's party now," chattered a cheerleader named Brandy Kurtz.

Lisa cut Brandy off with a steely glare.

"I heard Jojo invited Brent Tucker," giggled another of Lisa's gang.

"Forget Brent," Lisa hissed. "If you ask me, the only decent available guy right now is Eric Geraci."

Leanne floated on top of the talk, singing to herself like she was the bouncing ball for the rock singalong. Parties. Clothes. Pop quizzes. Girls' volleyball. Sometimes Leanne wondered if Crescent Bay High had anything to do with the real world. It certainly had nothing to do with her. Everyone was so frantic over being invited to some absurd party, while Leanne

doubted that many people would notice if she
never showed up at school again. She'd eaten
lunch alone since freshman year. She'd been
"off camera" for every yearbook. The school
attendance computer wouldn't even be able
to reach her since she'd moved out of her mother's house and was living on her own in a rented
room.

Leanne threaded her way through groups of
preppies, groups of jocks, groups of drama
nerds, groups . . . groups . . . groups . . . As
she passed the clumps and cliques, Leanne imag-
ined the kind of gossip she could indulge in with
her nonexistent friends.

*Now that I have a glamorous job washing dishes
at the Tucker Resort, do you think I can pay my rent?
Maybe I should tell you all what I put up with just
to keep my job there. Of course I could always go
back to my mother and her boyfriend and take my
chances on another black eye. Oh, you thought that
last shiner was just weird makeup? You're kidding!*

Leanne could guess that people did talk about
what a weirdo she was. Part of her was proud
of being weird and made a point of being even
weirder, while another part of her wanted to fade
into the walkways on the roped-off quad. Coast-
ing through the hall, Leanne ran a beat in her

head until her own locker came into view and the thudding of her heart took over as the drums. Jojo Popularity was at her locker, which was right next to Leanne's. Jojo, dressed in yellow culottes and matching polo shirt, was making her long-haired guy friend wait while she did little leaps and waved.

Leanne rarely smiled, and she wasn't about to fall down on her knees and change her ways for Jojo. Just because she had given Jojo one piece of advice, and talked once to Jojo's friend, Kat, Jojo was suddenly acting like she and Leanne were members of the same social club.

"Hi, Leanne!" Jojo cheered.

Leanne girded herself, striding up, and pretending that Jojo and the hippie blond guy weren't even there.

Jojo turned her cheerleader smile on Leanne. "You know Chip Kohler, don't you?" Jojo asked.

Leanne stared while Chip nodded in an easy, nonthreatening way. His ponytail was tied with a leather lace. A pair of glasses hung from a cord around his neck, over a sloppy T-shirt that read *BE HAPPY*. Finally, he smiled, too, but his smile was totally different from Jojo's. It carried no requirement to smile back.

"Hi," Leanne muttered, then began spinning her lock.

"Hi," Chip said with a shrug.

Leanne dared to open her locker while Jojo and Chip were still standing there. They could see her collection of towels and vitamins, shampoo and instant soup — a survival kit for days when her rooming house had no hot water or heat. Jojo had discovered that Leanne was living on her own. But she hadn't blabbed about it — at least Leanne didn't think she had.

Jojo stared after Leanne for a moment. Leanne's coolness got to her in a way that she didn't like or quite understand. Then she went back to Chip. "So what do I do?" Jojo asked him. "I've already invited both Kat and Gabe and now they're suddenly not speaking to each other. What if one of them refuses to come because the other one is going to be there? I tried to find Kat right after school to ask her if it was going to be a problem, but she'd already gone down to the public pool for her workout."

"Gabe and Kat will be cool," Chip promised.

Jojo stared at the list posted inside her locker door. There must have been fifty names, and Leanne knew that they were all people who had been invited to Jojo's now-famous party. The top five names were underlined in red. Leanne tried not to stare, but at the same time she was mesmerized by the idea of being on speaking terms with that many people.

Jojo stood on tiptoe and checked the underlined names on the top of her list, which Leanne saw at second glance were also marked with red and silver stars. "What about Miranda and Eric?"

"What about them?" Chip responded.

Jojo chewed her lip. "I finally decided to invite both of them. How can I have a decent party without inviting Eric Geraci?"

Chip didn't answer.

"What was I supposed to do? I don't know if Miranda will even be able to come," Jojo huffed. "I tried to call her all weekend, but her dad wouldn't let me talk to her. I looked for her again during lunch today, but who knows where she went. The least she could do is find me at lunch just once and let me know what's going on."

Chip glanced over at Leanne, meeting her gaze for a split second. His soft brown eyes made her think of a child or a stuffed toy. "Don't worry about it so much," he stressed. "It's just a party, Jo, not the solution for world peace."

Leanne smirked.

Jojo frowned, an expression that Leanne hadn't seen very often on the cheerleader. The smile queen in a darker mood.

"I know it's just a party," Jojo said, leaving her lists for a moment and examining her pretty face in the mirror that hung on the locker's back wall. Jojo's frown turned to a pout, as if Chip had betrayed her by making her face the truth. She picked out a few books, then took the rest of Chip's load and shoved it back inside her locker. "I just want it to be special," she said in a sadder voice. "I want my party to make a difference, about lots of things." She closed her locker door. "I thought you were helping me, Chip. I thought you were on my side."

"I'm always on your side," Chip answered with a thoughtful, slightly fed-up sigh and another glance at Leanne. "I'm always on everyone's side."

"Well, good," Jojo grumped. She took a deep breath, and without a good-bye to Leanne, rushed off.

After Jojo was gone, Leanne slowly picked through her belongings. Chip was still standing there. He looked around thoughtfully, frowning as if he were figuring out a math problem. When she finally had her books and was ready to head off campus, he suddenly tapped her shoulder.

"Hey, like, want to come to a party?" He pulled a folded pink invitation out of the pocket of his baggy pants.

"What?" Leanne stammered, wondering if he'd meant it as an insult or a joke. She could have cursed herself for starting to blush, but she could feel her milky-white skin getting splotchy and hot.

Chip slipped on his glasses to check the invitation before giving it to her. His specs were square, tortoiseshell: kind of nerdy, especially against the background of his sweet face and all that blond, beautiful hair. He held the invitation out to her. When Leanne still didn't take it, he explained, "I'm helping, so I guess I can, like, help invite people. I guess I can do something for once. Here."

Who are you trying to kid? Leanne thought. "I probably have to work that night. I work weekends at the Tucker Resort."

"Check and see," Chip responded in a soft voice. He looked thoughtful again and smiled. "If you feel like it, drop by."

Leanne wondered if he really meant, drop dead. But he still wore that easygoing smile, and she knew better then to say anything more. Fi-

nally she took the invitation from him and stuck
it in her English book. Then she nodded her
head, smiled back a millisecond grin that felt
more like a nervous tick, and walked away.

Tiny waves broke in the aquamarine water of
the Crescent Bay Public Pool.

Kat watched them at eye level, listening to the
low roar echoing off the high ceiling. She loved
her workouts in the tile-lined cave. It was her
refuge, her isolation tank. Her tight swim cap,
nose plug, and goggles made her feel like she
was in a cocoon. Kat often stayed so late that
she would be there after all the other swimmers
had gone home.

But even as Kat porpoised up and down, she
couldn't shake the unnerving feeling that something had gone terribly wrong. She was headed
over to Miranda's after her swim, but that wasn't
worrying her. Actually she was delighted to finally have some time with her best friend again.
Gabe was the problem. She and Gabe were suddenly so far apart that sitting on either side of a
microphone now would be like yelling at each
other from separate planets.

What exactly had happened between them?
Gabe had never acted this way before. Always

jokey, teasing, as buddy-buddy with her as he was flirtatious with other girls, the two of them had made the perfect pair. Not as in *couple,* of course. Something else. Something strange and powerful and hard to define. Something Kat missed desperately now that they had broken up.

"Broken up!" Kat babbled underwater, her voice sounding like a cartoon character. "What am I thinking about? I am truly demented and should just go live alone in a hut. There was nothing to break up!" Thinking about Gabe was making her feel tired, even though she was kicking off for what had to be her second mile of laps.

Concentrating on the water again, Kat flopped over on her back. She watched the sprinkles of water fall from her fingertips. Then she rolled over into freestyle, put her head down, and really began to swim hard. Her body was like a torpedo now. Her kick came from the thighs, powerful and deliberate. She focused on her breathing. As she flew through the water and sensed the wall coming up, she got ready to pull in for her turn, then rocket off the side of the pool.

But just as she got to the wall and began her somersault, she felt a light tap on her slick, bare shoulder. It broke her rhythm, and she stopped.

When she looked up from under the surface of
the water, she saw the squiggly, blurry form of
a boy looking down at her.

Kat thought immediately of Gabe. Well, it
was about time that he showed up and apolo-
gized! Why he had ever overreacted to her teasing and given up their show was a mystery. And
a mistake. She tread water, staying under until
her lungs screamed for air. When she burst to
the surface, her eyes opened wide, burning from
the chlorine. She was ready for an explanation.

But it wasn't Gabe. Not at all.

It was Brent.

Brent was kneeling at the edge of the pool,
wearing a striped button-down shirt, a loosened
tie, and crisp white pants rolled up to the knees;
he looked as if he were going to a formal clam
dig. He tested the water with his fingertips, then
flicked droplets off his palm, making his expen-
sive watch rattle.

Kat scrambled to tug off her nose clip and cap.
With all the rubber pressing against her makeup-
less face, she wondered if she was covered with
indentations, a face like a jigsaw puzzle.

He sat all the way down and smiled. Two
dimples dug into his smooth cheeks, making his
elegant face look softer and younger. There was

something new in his calm, blue eyes. A touch of neediness, or maybe it was just confidence.

"I was just driving by," he said.

"You seem to drive by a lot of places these days."

He shrugged. "I remembered hearing that the swim team held their meets here."

"We're not competing now," Kat said, holding onto the side of the pool as if it were a life raft. Half of her was safely underwater, while the other half was suddenly covered with goosebumps. She felt naked and began to tremble. "We're just training."

He dipped his bare feet in, splashing softly. "Actually I didn't come to see a swimming race." He looked at her. His eyes were almost the color of the safe, comforting pool water. "I came to see you again."

She wrapped her arms across her chest. "Hi."

He sighed, an earnest, painful sigh. Then he held up his hands as if he were only going to explain this one more time. "Kat, I've done everything I can to prove myself to you. I'll say it one last time. I was a jerk. You told me to announce it on the school PA; well, didn't I practically do that in the auditorium? By the way, I now think that Lisa's a jerk, too. This is my last try. I don't think I can do anything else. If you say go away now, I'll take you at your word. Just do me a favor, though. Don't you be a jerk, too. Say something!"

Kat didn't know if she could form a single syllable. No jokes were in her head, no witty comebacks. She thought of Lisa. She thought of all those crazy flowers. She thought of Brent standing up for Miranda. She thought of Gabe and how he had deserted her as she stared at Brent's refined face. Which way should she go? No or yes? Stop or go? Hold everything back or fly over the edge?

Kat was starting to get the feeling that she wasn't just standing in water, she was made of water. Her mind felt gooey, and her legs were weak. She defiantly flopped over on her back and kicked away from him, racing through the water.

But there was no getting away from it. Soon she was back at his end of the pool again. Brent was still perched on the tile, almost like a racer waiting to take off. "I like your swimming style," he said, rolling up his shirt sleeves. "You look really aggressive in the water. Kind of like a shark."

"Is that a compliment?" Kat managed. "I bet you know a lot about sharks."

"Maybe I do."

Before Kat could say anything else, he whipped off his watch, stood up, pointed his arms, and did a perfect three-point dive with all his clothes on! Kat watched with amazement as he entered the water and swam under her, his shirt flapping, his tie streaming, and his pants sticking to his legs. When he came up, he grinned and flipped a spray of water from his wet hair. He looked innocent and sweet, like a kid who'd been thrown off the boat at summer camp.

"YOU'RE CRAZY!" Kat shouted, looking around for the lifeguard. Her voice rang and echoed back at her. She and Brent were totally alone.

"Crazy about you," he gloated, starting to dog-paddle around her.

She swam away from him. "No."

"Yes," he teased.

"NO!"

"YES!!!"

Then he grabbed her foot, and Kat struggled, hearing another low, echoey noise bouncing off the walls. It took her a moment to recognize the

sound. She was laughing! Kat flopped under the
water and grabbed his knees. There was no more
indecision.

Brent swam away from her, so she glided back
and forth in front of him like a shark, now,
humming the *Jaws* theme. *"Dunh dun, duhn dun,
duhn dun . . ."*

"You'll never catch me," Brent teased.

"Oh, yeah?" she dared, connecting with a person she hadn't been for a long time. The person
who was so alive and daring that she felt like
she could get away with anything. Still laughing,
Kat dove under the water, otterlike, until she
caught hold of the back of Brent's shirt.

"Help! Lifeguard!" Brent yelled in a fakey fal-
setto. He flipped over, reached for her, and
tugged her under.

"BREEENNNNT!" she yelled out, then
closed her mouth before she went under the surface. When she emerged, she wiggled away desperately, but Brent went after her, and he didn't
let her go. Instead he held her firmly and looked
into her face. He didn't smile this time, and he
didn't dunk her. Things became very quiet. Just
the tiny waves lapping against the sides of the
pool.

"You know, you're a mystery," Brent whispered.

"*I'm* a mystery?" Kat questioned.

"Shhhh." He put a finger to her lips, then very gently lowered his face to hers. Kat knew exactly what was happening. She'd pictured this the minute he'd dived into the pool. His nose was brushing past hers. Water drops fell across her face. The slickness of his wet skin suddenly made Kat go weak and then his lips were on hers.

She was kissing him back, no more thoughts of leaving or blaming and living alone in a hut. This was every pore of skin on sensory overload. Wet, heavy cloth. Drippy hair. The sharp taste of chlorine. Kat didn't know whether she was shivering cold or just warm and dizzy. All she knew was that she'd made her move, and there was no turning back now.

SEVEN

"Kat."

"I know, I know."

"Do you?"

"Okay, Miranda. I don't know for sure. But how does anyone really know for sure? Maybe I don't want to think about it. I can't think anymore. All I know is how I feel."

"How do you feel?"

"I feel fantastic. I feel outrageous, like jumping up and down a thousand times and singing to the moon. I feel like Brent is an amazing person. I feel the way you probably feel about Jackson."

"SHHH!"

For about the fifth time that afternoon, the chatter between Miranda and Kat had suddenly stopped, replaced by silence, a glance toward Miranda's bedroom door, then a hug and tearful relief over being able to share their lives again.

"I can't believe that we've barely been able to see each other when we've both been going through such major life bizarreness," Kat cried after she'd climbed back up on Miranda's four-poster bed.

Miranda curled up on the rug and nodded.

"The last few weeks have been (a) crazy; (b) traumatic; (c) incredible; and (d) all of the above," Kat sighed.

"I really do think it's great about you and Brent," Miranda whispered, trying to talk herself into it. She wanted Brent to be great for Kat's sake. But she also wanted Kat to say right back to her, *Jackson's great, too. You did the right thing. You did, you did, you did!*

"You should have seen the way Brent stood up for you," Kat informed her. "I'm not sure when I'm going to see him again. Before we left the pool, he mentioned watching the girls practice volleyball this weekend on the beach. And Jojo's party. I told Jojo to invite him, so I'll definitely see him again there."

Miranda nodded. "At least I get to go to Jojo's party, too. My dad said he'd let my punishment end at seven-thirty next Saturday night. So I can go to Jojo's and after that, I'm free!"

"Really? Jojo's going to be so happy! I can't wait to tell her that you can come. I think she's been feeling kind of left out."

Miranda tried to be excited, too, but Jojo's party was just one more thing to worry about. "My dad said he's ungrounding me in time for the party because I agreed to talk to Eric today."

At the mention of Eric's name, Kat crumpled down on the mattress as if she'd been shot dead. "Oh." She turned over and put her chin in her hands. "I still can't believe it about you and Jackson. I can't believe that you two don't still hate each other."

"Maybe there's a fine line between love and hate," Miranda said.

"I think I know what you mean."

There was a knock at the door. Kat sat up. Miranda grabbed an algebra book and stuck it up to her face.

Mr. Jamison barely looked in. Through a tiny crack, he announced, "Eric's here," then stomped back down the hall. Miranda felt like she could hear the keys swinging from his hip.

"Speaking of people you love and hate," Miranda whispered, covering her face with her hands. She wondered if she'd ever have the nerve to tell her father the truth. He was still demanding that she be the old predictable Miranda, who studied so hard and took on so many school activities that she never had time to wonder. Little did her dad know that when he'd sentenced her to her lonely room, he'd made her do the one thing she hadn't had time to do in her overly busy sixteen years.

Think about herself.

Miranda had thought so much that her brain was on overload. She'd really looked at herself, but she had no idea who she'd seen. She used to be so sure about everything, as if her life were a map and all she had to do was follow the dotted lines. Now she could barely take a step without wondering if it was in the right direction.

"Do you love or hate Eric?" Kat asked as she pulled on her sweatshirt.

"I realized that I never felt strongly enough about Eric to love or hate him," Miranda sighed. "We dated each other for over a year. I think we went out every single Saturday night, and I don't even miss him now that we've broken up."

"The truth is always scary, I guess." Kat put her boots back on and collected her funky gym bag. Suddenly she took off the old rabbit's foot Miranda had given her so long ago and handed it over. "Just remember, if you can judge by

crazy me. Today is the day when things start
looking up. Good luck."

Miranda hooked the rabbit's foot chain around
her belt loop. "Thanks."

Before Kat left, they hugged one last time,
resting their foreheads together as if they were
trading thoughts. Finally Kat gave Miranda a
thumbs up and slipped out the door.

Alone again, Miranda stared at her mirror,
which was framed by all her reminders and rib-
bons. Old tutoring appointments. Schedule for
Friends In Need, the peer counseling program
for which she was training as a counselor. It all
felt like such a joke now. Together Miranda. Ha-
ha. She was the one who needed someone to talk
to, someone to tutor her in what she was supposed to do.

Dragging a brush through her hair, Miranda
thought about her life before the Turnaround
Formal. Everyone had always thought of her as
such a hard worker, but it hadn't been hard at
all. Living life on a schedule was easy! Stepping
into the unknown, now *that* was hard. That was
scary.

The only thing Miranda had figured out for
certain during her days alone was that she wasn't
as brave as she would have liked to be. When

she'd run out on Eric and into Jackson's arms, she'd thought she was taking a courageous leap into freedom. But now she was afraid she'd flung herself off the edge of the earth. She knew that Jackson wasn't afraid of landing anywhere or crashing on his head. But she was caught, desperately flapping her wings in midair.

Knowing that she couldn't keep Eric waiting any longer, Miranda marched slowly down the steep central staircase, as if she were about to face a firing squad. By the time she reached the bottom of the stairs, her heart was skipping beats. Her hands were shaking. The back of her neck was damp.

Eric was standing with his back to her, in front of the huge picture window that looked out over the ocean. The glare of the orange sunset was so bright that at first all Miranda could do was blink.

Eric slowly turned around. Backed by the fiery light and faint pounding of the waves, he looked like an expressionless judge, instead of the friendly, all-American jock she'd dated so many weekends. His jeans were immaculate. His cowboy boots looked spit shined. Under his letter jacket he wore a red plaid shirt that Miranda had never seen before. He stood with his hands

in his pockets, the expression on his face so controlled that it might as well have been a mask.

"Hello," Miranda said, her voice sounding
like it was coming from someone else.

He didn't look at her. "Hello."

They stood for a few moments while the surf
moved in and out. Finally Miranda moved to
the chair by the wooden coffee table. Eric ambled
to the small love seat. They sat down, their knees
buckling at exactly the same time.

"Thanks for coming over," she managed after
a long pause.

Eric tried to rearrange his legs, which were
way too long for the rattan love seat. Then he
began jiggling his knee and looking around the
house as if he'd never been there before.

Miranda looked around, too. Her beachfront
house was a prize-winning design. The whole
first floor was open and visible from the balcony
above, where she suddenly noticed her father
sitting with one arm on the rail, looking over a
legal brief.

"Well," Eric said.

"Yes?" Miranda blurted out at the same time,
glancing up at her father.

Eric folded and unfolded his broad athlete's

hands. He flashed her an angry look. "Are you going to explain?"

Miranda had tried to explain. Before the dance, she'd tried to tell Eric that she couldn't exist according to his whims and rules. But he hadn't wanted to listen. "I know I owe you an apology," she recited. "I'm sorry. I walked out on you and that was a horrible thing to do."

Eric barely moved. "That's all you have to say?"

She glanced up at her father again.

Finally Eric looked at her. For the first time she saw real sadness in his brown eyes. She could almost picture stoic, manly senior Eric with tears running down his cheeks.

"That's all you have to say after leaving me in the ballroom, looking like a total fool?"

How could she explain that she couldn't appear with him as Princess and her Shining Knight because it would have been such a lie. They weren't an ideal couple. They never had been. Under all the achievement and the neat looks were two people who had never tried to understand one another. "I'm sorry, Eric. I'm still not totally sure why I did it, but I'm sorry that you were hurt."

"There's just one thing I want to know," he said in a softer voice. He looked down at his hands. "Is there some other guy?"

The blood rushed to Miranda's face, and she was too dizzy to answer.

"I didn't think there was," Eric decided. "But for a while, people were talking. I told them you would never do something like that."

Miranda barely breathed.

"I know you wouldn't start seeing some other guy without breaking up with me first."

After that both of them watched the waves while a colorful kite fluttered on the deck. Finally Eric stood up. "I should go home and study." He shrugged and dug his hands into his letter jacket. "I guess it's good to see you again. Maybe now it won't be so weird when we run into each other at school."

"I don't want it to be weird," Miranda said, reaching for his hand without really thinking about it.

He grasped her hand back. "I don't, either. I just . . ."

When Eric's voice died out, Miranda walked him to the door, holding his hand the whole way because it was such a familiar, easy gesture. Meanwhile a hard lump had formed in her throat. She waited until they'd reached the door to draw up her nerve.

"I should tell you one thing, though . . ." she said, as he opened the door.

His eyes widened, and his eyebrows raised.

Miranda took a breath and tried to tell him. She wanted to tell him about Jackson. She wanted everything to be out in the open and under control again. But then she heard the footsteps of her father as he began trotting down the stairs.

"What?" Eric prodded.

Miranda glanced at her father. "I'm sorry," she muttered. "That's all, I guess." She backed away from Eric and rushed past her father on her way back upstairs. "I'm sorry, I'm sorry, I'm . . ."

EIGHT

Plop.

Plop plop.

Plop plop plop.

Plop . . . oooooomph. . . .

"Yeah, Sea Lions. GO! GO! GO! GO! GO!"

Applause and whistles broke out across the beach. The Crescent Bay High girls' varsity volleyball squad had just scored another point during their Saturday practice game. The Mendocino Crusaders were only one point ahead of the Sea Lions.

But not everybody watching the game was interested in who was winning. Brent Tucker, for one, couldn't care less about volleyball. His interest was watching the *crowd* watching the volleyball game. That's why he was above the beach, on the promenade, sitting on the stone wall, and eyeing Kat and Jojo, who were enthusiastically cheering on the team.

Brent shaded his eyes. No one had noticed him from down below. If they looked up toward the promenade, they undoubtedly would see him as just another Crescent Beach tourist. That was fine by him. He liked planning, and he liked calculating his next move. That's what he was doing right now. He could see Kat — pretty in the afternoon light of the beach — and her crowd. They used to look as tight as any clique that Brent had ever seen. But now Miranda was missing. Gabe and Kat sat on opposite sides of the net. Brent smiled. He had seen lots of other cliques come flying apart. He didn't hedge his bets on any group of friends.

No, he liked to fend for himself. He navigated the social waters of high school just like a shark would navigate the waters of the ocean. That's what he was doing right now. Trying to navigate, trying to second-guess. He'd had a great time wooing Kat back again. He'd taken flowers from the resort decorator, knowing it would break Kat down. He'd written notes, which were so much easier than making actual appearances. He'd stood up for Miranda at the school assembly, knowing that Kat would respond. It was all his way of trying to get Kat to trust him again.

He'd also thrown Kat off guard at the swimming pool. He'd done it deliberately. When Kat was at her most relaxed and private, he'd snuck into the pool and confronted her. He'd made Kat have fun. She was still suspicious; she still hadn't quite trusted him. But in the swimming pool the two of them had laughed and played like kids. After that Brent knew there would be no more problem of Kat trusting him again.

Plop plop . . .

Plop plop plop . . .

Brent chuckled to himself. Kat's heart was a little bit like that volleyball. It got bounced one way, then another. Brent thought that was just fine as long as he was doing the bouncing.

He fully intended to keep right on doing that. He'd ask her out again, and she'd go. He'd go out with her one or two more times. After that he'd know that he and Kat could part friends. She wouldn't try to get back at him. She wouldn't try to smear his reputation when he went on to bigger and better things at Crescent Bay High.

Maybe they'd even both enjoy it. Until he got bored. She certainly seemed to be putty in his hands after the swimming pool, which was usually the beginning of boredom as far as Brent was concerned. He knew if he just walked down from the promenade and onto the beach, Kat would spot him and she'd run right over. She'd want him to come over and be part of their crowd. The others wouldn't know what to make of him. They'd be a little suspicious at first, too, especially Gabe. But they'd get over it, just like Kat got over it.

Brent turned away from the volleyball game. He looked down the promenade toward his dad's resort hotel. Its big, modern imposing shape dominated the Crescent Beach skyline.

Frankly, the volleyball game was beginning to bore him, too. But there was one person who didn't bore him. He had no idea where he stood with her and wasn't sure if he would ever win her trust — Leanne Heard.

Brent began walking toward the resort. In a few minutes he was away from the sounds of the volleyball game, past the tourists riding their dopey pedal cars, and the hot dog stand shaped like a giant clam. He headed into the lobby. The tropical fish in the huge aquarium at the entrance seemed to wink at him in conspiracy, but Brent didn't stop to look. Instead he went straight back to the main kitchen.

The doors swung open, and he smelled soup cooking, heard the voices of the cooks, and saw the steam rising from the pots on the gas stove. Brent didn't bother to slow down. The girl he was looking for would be in the back, making salads or washing dishes. He'd only visited Leanne once before. Although he'd threatened and bullied her, she'd resisted him, which was what made him want to go back for a second try.

But when Brent got back to the dishwashing hole, Leanne was not to be found. John MacDiarmid, one of the restaurant busboys, was dumping plates into a plastic tub.

Brent nodded at him. "Have you seen Leanne?" he asked without much fanfare.

MacDiarmid was uncooperative at first, but finally he acknowledged Brent. "She's not here."

"Where is she?"

"She got off about a half hour ago."

"Do you know where she went?"

MacDiarmid looked like he didn't want to answer. "I think she went down to the beach," he muttered.

Brent took a step closer. MacDiarmid was looking down into a giant pot of soapy water.

Brent put his fingers into the water and suddenly flicked drops into MacDiarmid's face.

The busboy flinched. "Hey, what are you doing that for?"

"Because I don't talk to you for vague answers, you little wimp. Now if you want to keep working here, I suggest you tell me where Leanne went."

Brent waited. MacDiarmid wiped his T-shirt and then finally his arm across his forehead. "Okay. Okay. She went down to the beachfront arcade. She likes to hang out there."

Brent didn't say anything else. He was on his way.

"SPIIIIIIKE ITTTTTTT!"

"Boom boom boom it!"

"Punch it like a beach ball!"

Chip felt a nudge from Gabe, who was lying right next to him, stretched out on the sand. "Punch it like a *beach ball?*" Gabe questioned.

"Hey, don't knock it." Chip sat cross-legged and shifted his hips to make a more comfortable seat for himself. "You need a new partner for your radio show now. Maybe you should learn to appreciate my hidden wit."

"Your half wit."

"That, too."

"Who says I need a new partner, anyway?" Gabe answered. "Just forget my dumb radio show. It's a thing of the past."

Chip chewed on the frame of his glasses, which hung from the cord around his neck. "You're the one who's been talking about your show all week, Gabe. And you're the one who's in such a crummy mood."

Gabe sifted sand through his fingers, then glared at the other side of the net, where Kat and Jojo were cheering and jumping up and down like jack-in-the-boxes.

Gabe looked back at Chip. "I just thought Kat might have had second thoughts about canceling our show. But from what I can tell, she couldn't care less. She's sure in an all-time happy mood today." He shaded his eyes, glanced at Kat again, then looked up at the Tucker Resort.

"Maybe you should talk to her," Chip suggested.

"Chip, I don't need your sensitive-guy advice right now, okay?"

"Okay."

Finally Gabe sighed and sat up. "Sorry. I don't mean to take it out on you."

"It's cool." Chip went back to watching the

volleyball game. He wasn't bothered by Gabe's grumpiness. Usually Gabe was the upbeat go-getter while Chip fretted and asked advice. But the simple act of defying Jojo by asking Leanne Heard to her party had already made him feel a little stronger. When he'd told Jojo about it, she'd almost choked, and then she'd decided to let the invitation stand. Maybe for once in his life, he'd crossed that line that Gabe had talked to him about. Whatever the reason, Chip was feeling pretty good.

"POINT! POINT!"

"YES, YES!" Chip yelled as he shot to his feet. The last volley popped back and forth until Amy Zandarski spiked it with a fierce snarl and a fist like a big stone. The ball buzzed past a Mendocino player's nose, shooting into the sand.

That was it. The game was over, and Chip decided to scream his head off. "AAA-MEEEE, AAA-MEEEE!"

Soon everybody was bouncing up and down, and Gabe finally stumbled to his feet, too. Even the sea gulls seemed to join all the cheering while the team flowed off the court and mingled with the crowd.

Chip was dusting sand off his baggy pantleg when he saw that Gabe was finally pulling himself together. The comb had come out of Gabe's back pocket and, even though he kept casting long glances at Kat, he had begun to smile at Amy, too. Meanwhile Kat was gathering her things with Jojo, while Amy was wiping her face with a towel and casting a shy smile back at Gabe.

Hoping it would cheer Gabe up, Chip accompanied him over to where Amy was waiting. Amy's face was red and her hair was pulled back with two clips.

"Hi," Amy sighed, barely noticing Chip. Her Crescent Bay High jersey and shorts showed off a teeny waist and strong, slender legs.

"Amy, dudette," Gabe said, looking back at Kat again. His DJ voice projected across the beach. Sure enough, Kat turned back and stared.

Gabe watched Kat a little longer, then gently touched Amy's temple, catching a dribble of sweat.

Amy's face became even redder. She kicked at the sand. "Thanks for coming to our practice game. If we play like this we'll beat Watsonville next Thursday." She shrugged. "At least I hope we will."

"You will. And I'll be there to see it," Gabe grinned. "It blows me away how you can be this nice, normal junior at school and then turn into the queen of spike. Hey, maybe I can interview you about that . . ." He faltered, seeming to remember that he no longer had a show to interview her on. "At Jojo's party. I'll interview you there. Up close and personal."

Amy bit her lip as she tied her sweatshirt around her waist. "Um, actually, I don't think I've been invited."

"What?" Gabe reacted, almost knocking himself over. "Chip, do you hear that?"

Chip smiled.

"Of course you've been invited," Gabe carried on. He took Amy's arm and pretended to write on it, then nibbled on her knuckles. "There. You just got your invitation." Then he put his arm around Chip and smiled. "Chip has influence, so it's okay."

"Really?"

"Next Saturday night," Chip confirmed. "Eight o'clock. Be there."

"Oh . . . okay . . . yes," Amy stammered, but Chip had to offer the final nod because Gabe was already gone. Kat and Jojo were climbing over the stone promenade wall, heading away from the beach, and Gabe was jogging after them.

"We'll see you then," Chip blurted out as he

waved to Amy and ran, too. His best friend was
standing in the middle of the intersection, where
the prom met Ocean Avenue. Kat and Jojo were
gone.

Gabe began striding up the town's main drag.
Chip followed him past the noisy old beachfront
arcade. They walked by Ten Tiny Tees Minia-
ture Golf, two taffy stores, Captain Roger's Sea-
food Grotto, and the stand that sold "elephant
ears," which sent off a heavy smell of fried sugar.

"Gabe, man, like where are you going?" Chip
called, catching up to him between the Fudge
Company and the kite store. "My van's down
in the beach parking lot."

"Nowhere. Anywhere. As long as I'm not
near the Tucker Resort." Gabe threw his hands
up and made a U turn, heading just as furiously
back down to the beach. "I need to walk. I need
to think."

"You need to chill out, Gabe."

Gabe just shook his head and kept walking
until they were right back at the arcade. There
was a constant chorus of pings and squeals,
roars, crashes, and snatches of electronic music.
The arcade entrance was dark and reeked of stale
popcorn. Between the tourists and the locals
who hung out there, the place was packed.

But before Chip could figure out what to do about Gabe, he glanced through the arcade window. Inside the arcade, along with the greasy-haired kids who wore studded bracelets, Chip saw Leanne Heard. She was alone, wearing a silky thrift-store dress and a man's white T-shirt with the sleeves rolled up. A long scarf was tied around her wrist and it fluttered as she played pinball.

While Gabe fretted, Chip stared. Leanne fascinated him, and he wasn't sure why. He was Mr. Natural, and yet he liked her hair, which was as artificially white as a baby doll's. He related to that scared sadness in her gray eyes and the way she always seemed to be looking over her shoulder.

He pointed her out to Gabe. "That's the girl I invited to Jojo's party. You don't know her very well, do you?"

Gabe was too preoccupied to care.

And that was when Chip saw Brent Tucker, slicing his way through the arcade crowd. Since Brent had only been at Crescent Bay High for a few weeks, Chip barely knew him. But he did know that it was weird for a rich preppie to hang out at the grimiest of Crescent Bay dives.

Chip put his glasses on, stepping close to the

window, and straining to see past the shifting,
clumpy crowd. He was astounded to see Brent
shove a kid to the ground as he headed for
Leanne. When Brent reached Leanne's pinball
machine, he shook it hard, making her jerk her
head to one side — bits of platinum hair sticking
to her painted mouth. When Chip saw the
expression on Leanne's face, he began to move.

Forgetting about Gabe, Chip made his way
into the arcade. The floor was sticky, the crowd
was stubborn, but for once Chip didn't stop to
say Excuse me, So sorry, or Oops. He just kept
his bespectacled eyes on his destination and pried
his way through. People stepped on his feet and
laughed hot breath in his face, but he finally
made it over to the row of old-fashioned pinball
machines along the wall.

When Chip got there, Brent was squeezing
Leanne's arm, pulling her against him with such
force that her face twisted up with pain.

"What's the problem? I just came to find you
because I wanted to talk," Brent was wooing in
a sugary voice, while his hands were doing
something very different.

Leanne glared and tried to twist loose.

Chip took off his glasses. He had visions of
being a long-haired Clark Kent, but he was mo-

mentarily stuck without a phone booth or that last bit of nerve. Then he saw tears fill Leanne's eyes, and he shouted so loudly that his voice scraped against his throat.

"LEAVE HER ALONE!" Chip yelled.

Stunned, Brent took his hands off. But when he turned and saw Chip, he didn't seem to know who he was. "Back off, freak," Brent threatened. "This is between her and me."

That was when Gabe appeared. Brent had a different reaction when he saw Gabe. He let Leanne go and smiled.

Now Gabe was the violent-looking one. At the sight of Brent, his jaw tensed, his fist tightened, and the veins on his neck began to stand out. Chip wondered if he was going to have to protect Brent against his best friend.

"Hey, Gabe," Brent said with a funny laugh. "Good to see you, man." Brent backed away from Leanne with a cool smile.

Gabe glared. "I wish I could say the same," he said threateningly.

"Hey, I was just delivering a message from my dad to his employee," Brent said. "Leanne works in the resort kitchen, and there've been some problems at work. I don't know why my dad makes me do his dirty work." Shaking his head at Leanne, Brent smiled again and backed into the crowd.

After Brent was gone, Leanne turned away. She leaned over the pinball machine as if she were going to collapse.

"I knew that guy was bad news," Gabe exploded. "I knew it. I knew it!" He slammed his fist into his other hand.

Chip stepped toward Leanne. His hand reached out, but he didn't have the courage to touch her. "What happened? Are you okay?"

"Nothing happened," Leanne whispered. "Please go away."

Chip didn't budge until Gabe furiously yanked at his sleeve. Just as they turned to go, Leanne looked up at him with those amazing gray eyes again. But before he could say anything else, she went back to the pinball machine and began playing it like a pro.

NINE

"So Miranda is really going to go?"

"I'm sure she'll go, for Jojo's sake."

"Jojo will have a cow if her good friends don't all show up. And everyone *will* show up, just for Jojo."

"Well, Jojo's that kind of girl. She cares so much about her friends. She's always there if you need to talk. She'd never put herself or some guy ahead of her friends."

"She's so nice."

"To everybody."

To *everybody!* When Lisa Avery heard those words on Monday, she wanted to scream. It was fourth period, and she was in gym class. All around her on the polished wood floor of the gymnasium she could hear the squeak of aerobic shoes, and the talk of her classmates: *Party, party.*

*Jojo, Jojo . . . Jojo's crowd this, Jojo's crowd that,
yak, yak, yak.*

"Lisa, catch!"

Lisa looked up and saw a basketball flying at
her. She managed to put out her hands, but the
ball bounced off her palms and went *kerplunk* to
the floor. That set off a mad scramble by the rest
of the girls to grab it.

Lisa held back. She didn't like mad scrambles
either for basketballs or party invites. And she
certainly wasn't going to scramble just to join
in the talk about Saint Jojo. As far as Lisa was
concerned, Jojo was one of those junior girls
who was too insecure to threaten her friends by
getting a decent guy. She thought it was pathetic
that Jojo had five thousand admiring buddies and
zero hot dates.

But it was more than that. Jojo was also part
of the Miranda crowd. Lisa was still stinging
over being overlooked at the Turnaround
Dance. Maybe Miranda was smart and in clubs
and all that, but Lisa was a senior, so that had
been her very last chance. On top of everything,
two-faced Brent Tucker had made Lisa look like
a fool at that KHOT show for just pointing out
the obvious.

Whoosh . . .

Lisa turned around. Amy Zandarski had dropped a two-point shot from the outside perimeter of the court. So Amy was an athlete and a junior who would be even better next year. Goody for her. Basketball was so sweaty and disgusting anyway, and the goal was so dumb. Who really cared whether you put an orange ball through a net?

A shrill whistle pierced Lisa's thoughts. "Okay, girls, that's it for today. Everybody hit the showers."

A few minutes later and Lisa was out and dressed, but trying to ignore the continual gossip over Jojo's party. By the time she got out of the locker room, she felt semi-desperate. Okay. She was no athlete, no cheerleader, no perfect friend, class officer, brain, or radio personality. But she *was* a senior with a great body, street smarts, and a list of male admirers longer than the honor roll. That's what would distinguish her, even if she never got crowned prom queen or got accepted at Stanford or Yale.

With that in mind, Lisa headed straight for lunch. The cafeteria was still being remodeled, but most upperclassmen were hanging out on the quad because it was a positively gorgeous day. Telling herself that she was just as spec-

tacular, Lisa rearranged her leather skirt and
Spandex top, smeared on an extra pinkie of
candy-cane-flavored lip gloss, and went to
work.

"ERIC GERACI! ERRRRRRRICCCCC!"
she called out, so that no one in the quad had
any question about who she was looking for.
There were head turns and wolf whistles that
bolstered her as she pranced over bodies, making
her way toward a group of senior jocks who
surrounded Eric like bodyguards for his broken
heart.

Eric was sitting at the end of the table, almost
hidden under a tree. His big hands were holding
his letter jacket and a pile of books. As usual
these days, he had that beaten-down look.

"Eric, Eric how are you?" Lisa gushed in a
loud voice. The hammering and sawing in the
nearby cafeteria was making a racket. "I want
to ask you something. Come over where we can
hear each other."

Eric left his buddies and went with her, the
crowd naturally parting as he passed. Lisa
dragged him all the way off the quad and next
to the bike racks, where it wasn't nearly as noisy.
Stopping, she did a little trip over herself so that
Eric had to catch her.

"Good thing one of us is coordinated around here," she giggled.

Eric smiled briefly, his handsome face and brown eyes looking not altogether displeased.

Good, Lisa thought, this should be a snap. "Anyway," she plunged ahead, "I've been looking for you all day."

"You have?" Eric looked shocked that any girl would be looking for him, as if Miranda were the only female left on the planet.

"Of course. I heard that you've been down, and I wanted to see if I could help. What's going on?" *As if she didn't know*.

Eric shook his head. He looked back at the dumpster outside the cafeteria, full of old linoleum and smashed-up countertops. "School's weird. Senior year is weird. I don't know what's going on. What can I say?"

"Maybe I can explain a thing or two," Lisa invited, leaning back against the bike rack and gazing at him. "Maybe I can help get your senior year back on track."

He shook his head and laughed sadly.

"What's so funny?" she teased. She stretched out her leg and tapped his foot with hers. "Okay, look, Eric. Let's stop playing games. I know what your problem is. Everyone does."

Eric looked alarmed and embarrassed.

"Don't worry about it," Lisa soothed. "You're hardly the first guy to get dumped at this school. I'm sorry if I embarrassed you by mentioning it at that KHOT show in the aud, but you can't ignore it. You just need to get back on your feet."

"How am I supposed to do that when I can't stop thinking about Miranda?" he answered in a dull voice. "I just keep wanting to get back together. She told me there isn't another guy and I believe her, so maybe we *can* get back together. I don't know. I never see her at lunch. I think she's avoiding me."

Uh-oh. This was more complicated than Lisa had expected. She sighed and shook the anklet on which she had had engraved the name of her most recent guy. The current inscription was Ron Siebert, the college dork she'd taken to the Turnaround Formal. Talk about past tense.

The leg shake got Eric to look at her again, and when she smiled, he managed to smile back. "Maybe you need to get Miranda's attention," she advised.

Eric gave her a blank look. "How?"

"By letting her know that she's not the only person in your life."

"Huh?"

Lisa had to restrain herself from stomping on his toe. Guys could be such jugheads sometimes! "I just heard that Miranda is going to Jojo's party, and I'm sure that you've been invited, too. . . ."

He nodded.

"That's your big chance. At that party, you have to make Miranda think that you're not just pining away," Lisa lectured. "You have to have some spark. You have to show energy and interest. And you have to be seen with a very attractive girl."

There was curiosity in Eric's face now. And a touch of disbelief. "But what girl would want to go with me when all I want to do is talk to Miranda?"

"*Eriiic.* Do I have to spell it out for you?" Lisa licked her lips, then leaned forward and drew her finger along Eric's chin. "Now I know you're having a hard time, so I'll handle everything. You just leave all the planning to me."

Eric blinked. He looked off balance for a moment, but finally he nodded and smiled.

The note was written on pale blue stationery bordered in charcoal gray. The paper was so

elegant it might have been an invitation to the
White House rather than a love letter from
Brent.

> Kat:
> Yes, yes, yes, I'll watch the game with
> you this Thursday night in the gym. I love
> volleyball! I'm a lucky guy. Will you go
> to Jojo's party with me, only with me? Is
> it a date?
> Jaws

Jojo read over Kat's shoulder. School had just
finished for the day, and they were standing by
the activity bulletin board, the glass-covered case
filled with notices about meetings and clubs.
People also used the board to leave messages for
each other, and that's where Kat had found her
note from Brent, taped over an old notice about
the cafeteria remodeling and the KHOT live
show.

" 'Jaws?' " Jojo questioned.

Kat beamed, then put the note in her bag,
swinging it so the charms and bangles clinked.
"It's kind of a private joke, from when we
goofed around in the swimming pool. I can't
believe I got up the nerve to ask him to the

game," Kat drawled as Patty Prom Queen. She shook her head, making her hair fly straight out, then stamped her desert boots. "I feel so great! No more doubts. No more holding back. No more losers. No more bozos. Kat McDonough is back in the ring for good!"

Jojo stepped back. Kat was really hyper, even compared to Jojo, whose energy could usually fuel a major city. Jojo wanted to share Kat's glee, but Kat's good fortune was just another thing that made her feel like an old washrag. Good old Jojo. Nice, friendly Jojo. Jojo's locker was full of notes, but not one of them came close to being a love letter.

"What can I say?" Kat beamed. "It's a new day, it's a new life." She swung around a pole as she crossed the quad on her way off campus. "I used to pride myself on being so smart and clever on the radio. Now I sound like a greeting card."

Jojo followed, uncharacteristically silent.

"After last summer, I'd sworn off guys," Kat pronounced. Hanging from her necklace that day were a bunch of tiny plastic fruits and a whistle, which she blew, sending a loopy wail into the bright sky. "I was going to stay in my room every night until graduation . . . from college." She clapped her hands. "I guess things change."

For Jojo, nothing much was changing. Party or no party, she was still feeling like odd man out. In fact, she was feeling even odder. Miranda had finally called to say that she was coming to the party, but she still hadn't met Jojo for lunch or told her what was really going on. Meanwhile, Lisa was giving Jojo really nasty looks, and even Chip was starting to act distant.

What had Jojo done to deserve all that? She knew what she'd done to Lisa, of course, but what was Chip's problem? She'd generously gone along with his insane impulse to invite Leanne. Hey, she'd been nice to Leanne before Chip had ever gone into charity work. And once her party was in full swing, she planned to reconcile Kat and Gabe. She'd even get Eric and Miranda back on speaking terms if she had half a chance. She would give her party; give, give, give, be friendly, smiley Miss Congeniality until she was blue in the face. But what would be left in it for her? A few crackers and the leftover guys that no one else had time for?

When they neared the gym, Kat said goodbye, and Jojo doubled back across the quad, remembering that she had to pick up her pompoms for cheerleading practice. Trying to focus her mind on arm positions and pointy toes, she headed straight for her locker. She slowed down only when she saw Brent Tucker standing in front of it. He was the only figure in what was now a trash-strewn, deserted hall.

Jojo slowed down and even considered turning back.

Brent was wearing pleated trousers with a turtleneck and paisley suspenders. Impatiently he looked at his watch, then stared at her locker number.

As Jojo crept closer, she got a funny feeling. Sort of an upside-down stomach feeling, like the way she'd felt when she'd tried out for cheerleading squad. She stopped a few feet away from him, then realized that he wasn't really standing in front of her locker at all. He was standing in front of Leanne's locker.

"Excuse me," she whispered, reaching for her lock.

He seemed startled and flicked blond hair out of his eyes. A second later a warm smile appeared. He moved out of her way.

"Are you looking for Kat?" Jojo asked, unable to figure out any other reason why he would be hanging around. "I think she went to the pool."

"Kat?" he repeated, as if for a moment he'd forgotten who she was. "Oh," he remembered. "No. I wish I *was* waiting for Kat. Unfortunately I have to talk to someone who isn't nearly as fun as Kat. I'm looking for Leanne."

Jojo wanted to know more, but she controlled herself. "Oh. I'm Jojo Hernandez." She stuck out her right hand, which alone spelled out *ENT HI*. "I'm the one who invited you to my party. Kat's friend."

Brent grinned and bumped her with his shoulder. "I know. Everyone knows who you are. From what I hear, you're a very important person around this school."

Jojo giggled for no reason. She had never been this close to Brent, and now that she looked right into his face she saw that his eyes were the most amazing color of blue, like two panes of stained glass. He looked at her with such confidence and intensity.

Jojo started to get light-headed.

Brent glanced down and a lock of golden hair flopped over his forehead. "Thanks for inviting me. I know you must have thought I was a real loser when you saw me and Lisa together at the Turnaround Formal."

Jojo's mouth fell open. She'd never expected

Brent to bring up that subject on his own. "I . . . I . . . I . . ."

"It's okay." He held up his hand, on which he wore a thin, gold ring. "It was the biggest mistake of my life." He smiled again, and then very suddenly fell at Jojo's feet, as if he were praying to her.

Stunned, she inched away, but he jokingly clutched her around the hips.

"Please make sure Kat knows that I'm never getting near Lisa again," he pleaded in a half-kidding voice. "I'd just gotten to Crescent Bay High. But I'm not stupid. I never make the same mistake twice."

Jojo giggled again, more loudly this time. It felt as if a firecracker had just gone off inside. She was almost unable to stop laughing.

Brent finally stood up and put his hands in his pockets. He smiled at her, those blue eyes locking on again as two dimples dug themselves in his cheeks.

Jojo didn't know what to say. Her stomach wasn't just upside down now, it was flipping around and around like a washing machine. She faced her open locker and found her pom-poms. "So, um, what are you doing here, then? Why do you want to talk to weird Leanne?"

Brent sighed. "I'm sure Gabe told you what happened over the weekend . . ."

Jojo shook her head. Gabe and Chip had both acted weird that morning when she'd mentioned finally inviting Brent to her party. But she'd had to run to a spirit rally and hadn't hung around for an explanation.

"If they haven't told you yet," Brent explained, "I'm sure they will." He looked down the hall. "Do you know Leanne very well?"

"Not really."

"It's a mess," Brent sighed. He leaned toward Jojo, who leaned her ear toward him. "See, Leanne is working at my parents' resort. My dad didn't even want to hire her, but I told him she needed the job. I talked him into it."

"You did?"

Brent lowered his voice, his sleeve rubbing against Jojo's bare arm. "I don't quite know how to talk about this, but Leanne . . ." He paused and stared hard at Jojo. "You won't repeat this, will you?"

Jojo furiously shook her head.

"Okay. Well . . . Leanne . . . you know . . . she comes on to all the guys who work in the kitchen with her," Brent finally said, shaking his head in disgust. "Needless to say, a lot of guys

are only too happy to take her up on it, and it's
not real good for morale. Anyway, my dad is
mad about it. So I followed Leanne to that creepy
old arcade downtown, and I tried to warn her.
But she got so upset that she completely freaked
out. That's when your friends came in, too, so
I just left. She's nuts."

Jojo could barely control herself, she was so
riveted by Brent's story. It explained so much!
Before the Turnaround Formal, Leanne had told
Jojo that Brent was a sleaze. Well, who was the
sleaze now? And this was the girl Chip had invited to her party! Jojo made a mental note to
uninvite Leanne, Chip or no Chip.

Brent checked the hallway one last time.
"Look, I don't think Leanne is coming, so I'd
better go. Remember, you promised not to talk.
I don't want a lot of people knowing about this.
I know Leanne has a hard time, and I don't want
to make it any harder for her."

"I won't tell a soul," Jojo choked.

He started to leave, then turned back and
placed his palm on Jojo's forearm. She stared
down at his hand.

"You know, you are great to talk to." He
smiled. "I think a lot of people here assume I
have all these friends, because my parents own

this big resort. But I'm just like any other new guy." He still held onto her arm as he stared into her eyes again.

Jojo felt some strange kind of energy pass from his hand to her arm and all the way down her legs.

Finally he gave her a tiny squeeze and headed for the library.

Jojo buried her face in her pompoms. Her feelings of being ultra-nice and left out had disappeared. But what had replaced it was even scarier.

TEN

Unsuccessful decision-making strategies:
1. *Letting others decide for you.*
2. *Putting off thought and action.*
3. *Doing anything to avoid the worst possible result.*

Miranda stared at the band room blackboard while Mr. Newcomb, the counselor in charge of Friends in Need, continued printing with a squeaky piece of chalk. Sixth period, Thursday, this was the second workshop to train her as a peer counselor, so she could help other students with their problems. When Miranda was first chosen for Friends in Need, she hadn't been sure that she could really relate to people with problems. After all, her life was so tidy and together. Now she wondered if many Crescent Bay High students were as messed up as she.

She began writing again.

Successful decision-making strategies:
1. *Accepting responsibility.*
2. *Choosing to work for a positive outcome.*
3. *Devising a plan and following it.*

Miranda stopped copying Mr. Newcomb's list because she didn't want to think about decisions or plans. She looked around the room instead. Because Friends in Need peer counselors had been chosen from all Crescent Bay High social groups, there were a couple of jocks, a pair of nerds, debaters, soshes, preppies, brains, and even a few who were just plain odd. Where did she belong now, in her blazer and long skirt, her perfectly organized notebook opened atop her briefcase? All she knew was that she wanted to be with Jackson, who was lying on the band room floor, scribbling on a tiny pad.

"I'm glad that our new counselors-in-training came back for our second meeting," said Mr. Newcomb, who was youngish and wore an earring. He nodded to Jackson and a few others. "And I thank you experienced counselors for joining us and helping, too."

Jackson looked up. A pencil was behind his

ear, stuck between his dark hair and a blue bandana. Miranda hadn't been near him since lunch on Monday. When she didn't see him for more than a day, she would have trouble fixing his face in her mind, even though she never forgot a single detail of his touch.

Across the band room, she tried to look at him objectively. His jeans were so worn at the knees that there was nothing but thread. Instead of his leather jacket, he wore a big black sweater that was stretched out around the neck, a scarf, and lace-up leather boots.

"I'm going to pass out some worksheets, and then I want you to get into pairs — consisting of one new and one experienced counselor if possible," Mr. Newcomb instructed. "I want each pair to discuss the worksheet and fill it out."

Everyone grabbed at paper, then scrambled to find a partner. Without looking at Jackson, Miranda managed to be at his side in a matter of seconds. It was a new talent she'd developed, that of being inconspicuous and purposeful at the same time. When she got close enough, she wanted to slide her hand into his, but she dared only brush against his fingers. She was surprised when he didn't automatically glide away from the others to sneak off with her to some private corner. He made no move to leave the girl he was talking to, a skinny sophomore who wore a man's suit jacket so oversized that it came almost to her knees.

"Miranda, do you know Carin Greenberg?" Jackson said, in a bold, straightforward voice.

Neither Miranda nor Jackson had met any of each other's friends. Miranda stared down at her riding boots.

"Hi," Carin offered, smiling at Miranda. "I've heard you give speeches and stuff at school, but it's nice to actually meet you."

Miranda said nothing.

"Carin's been drawing cartoons for the paper," Jackson prompted. "We're going to print one in the next issue of *Bay News*."

Carin blushed and looked to Miranda for congratulations, but Miranda still didn't respond. She was growing so used to her solitary confinement that a normal conversation — especially with Jackson at her side — would be like screaming "Fire!" in a crowded building. Plus, Miranda didn't want to waste valuable time. Turning her back on Carin, she cast a long look at Jackson, then climbed up to the top of the band risers. She found a niche, where they would be hidden by a cello and a set of drums. Drawing up her skirt, she huddled and waited.

Jackson slowly trudged up the riser, taking an agonizingly long time to join her. When he folded down so that his knees touched hers, he didn't reach for her hand, even though no one would have been able to see. Of course, it was still too risky to kiss or embrace, but Miranda could tell that something else was stopping him. Something new was in his fierce, green eyes that reminded Miranda of earlier times, when all that passed between them had been suspicious and angry.

"What's wrong?" she asked as soon as he folded down next to her.

"You could have at least said hello to Carin," Jackson said. "She's on the newspaper staff."

"Jackson, this is practically our only chance to talk to each other," Miranda reacted. Her father had been working at home the last few days, so there was no sneaking around there. She and Jackson had still been meeting during lunch, but with less regularity. That coming Friday the next issue of *Bay News* would go to print. As the deadline grew close, Jackson had needed to spend more time in the journalism room. "I only got to go to this because it's during a class period. Otherwise my dad wouldn't have let me."

Jackson looked right at her. "Maybe you shouldn't pay so much attention to your dad."

Miranda felt like she had just fallen down a flight of stairs. What was she supposed to do? She'd always thought of herself as smart and strong, but she was her father's baby. When her mom had gone back to work, her father had cut back at his law firm to spend more time at home. Since she was little he'd made special efforts to take her to plays and lectures, to visit colleges and museums. The only time she'd ever defied him was the night she'd left Eric to run down to the beach with Jackson. Avoiding Jackson's glare, she pointed down at the worksheet. "We'd better do this assignment."

Jackson shook his head.

Mr. Newcomb's decision-making worksheet was entitled, *Making a decision. What's the problem? Hmmm?* was written on top, followed by a blank space to be filled in. Under that were three big circles, labeled *Alternative solutions 1, 2, and 3.* Each circle was divided in half, and there were spaces to fill in the positive and negative consequences of each solution.

Jackson boldly pressed his pencil down first, answering *What's the problem?* by writing in, *Us. Here and now.* Then he pointed to *Alternative so-*

lution 1 and handed the pencil over to Miranda. That old prove-yourself look was in his eyes.

Just wait for more time to pass, Miranda wrote in.

As soon as he read her words, Jackson grabbed for the pencil, but she held onto it and continued to write. *If we wait, Eric won't be so hurt. My father may change his mind about you.* She thought for a moment, then finally handed the pencil back.

Poised at *Negative consequences,* Jackson wrote without hesitation. *I don't believe in waiting. This is sick. This is wrong. This is a lie.* He went on to fill in the second alternative. *Go public right now!!* He glanced at her quickly, then went on to fill in *Positive consequences. It's real. It's right. You can't run from the truth.*

Miranda took her turn again. Her hand shook. She pressed down so hard with the pencil that the lead chipped away. *Negative consequences. My father will kill me. It will never work.*

When it came to the third circle, Jackson just drew in a huge question mark.

Miranda felt the pressure of tears. She wanted to grab the pencil and just scribble over the whole sheet, or rip it up and throw away the pieces.

Jackson finally sighed loudly, then grabbed her hands. "Let's sneak out together," he demanded in an urgent whisper. "I don't care where we go. We could go to the volleyball game tonight, or just out to the Wave. Anywhere, as long as there are other people there. Or how about Saturday night? Then you won't be grounded anymore."

"But that's the night of Jojo's party!" Miranda panicked. She could just imagine showing up at Jojo's with Jackson, when she'd made Eric think that there wasn't another guy. The idea made her sick. Besides, Jojo's party was when she planned to finally take Eric aside and explain. *Eric, I'm sorry. Eric, it happened. Eric, I fell in love with someone else.* As long as she told Eric before he found out on his own, she would feel like she'd been honest and up front. Then, once that hurdle was over, maybe she'd gather up her courage and introduce Jackson to her dad.

"We can't go to Jojo's together," she whispered. "NO."

"That's not what I'm talking about," Jackson insisted, leaning in so close that his face was almost touching hers. "There's a newspaper party that night, too, at Sarah's. Not many people will be there. Just my closest friends. Just make an appearance. Show up for half an hour. That's all I ask. It'll be a start."

"But how can I do that?" Miranda cried. "My father's dropping me off at Jojo's. He's picking me up, too. He won't let me go somewhere else."

"I'll figure it out," Jackson promised. "We have to do this. I'm telling you, Miranda. Everything I've ever learned has told me that you don't run away from things. If you do, they just blow up in your face."

"But . . ." Jackson touched her face, and she turned her head to kiss his hand before she'd even realized that she'd done it.

He smiled. "I'll figure it out, and then I'll leave you a note on the activity bulletin board." Jackson pointed down to his worksheet again. "We have a problem here, and Newcomb's right, we can't avoid it or let other people decide what we should do."

Miranda nodded, even though she didn't know if she had the guts to take another chance.

ELEVEN

That night, Gabe and Chip were standing down on the gym floor, only a few feet away from the serves and spikes of the volleyball game. The bleachers were packed. Neon lights flickered overhead. At almost halftime, the Sea Lions were displaying tight teamwork and lightning-fast moves, but Gabe was more concerned about another team that seemed to be getting tight and moving fast. Kat and Brent.

"Hey, Gabe . . ."

"Yeah."

"Look who just walked in. They finally got here."

"I see, Chip. Believe me, I see."

"Kat looks happy. Do you think she's really fallen for Brent? What do you think about what happened with Leanne?"

"I don't know. I just know that guy is a scumbucket."

Gabe's fists clenched, and his stomach turned rock-hard. Instead of her usual Boy Scout clothes, Kat was wearing a silky blouse, suspenders, and stiff, new-looking jeans, as if she'd gone out shopping especially for Brent. She seemed to hang on Brent, too, looking over her shoulder as he stood behind her, hands on her waist, guiding her up to the top bench.

Too disgusted to watch, Gabe faced the court again. Amy slugged a serve, and the volleyball popped back and forth. Jojo started a cheer where people stamped their feet and made the bleachers shake.

"SPIKE IT! SPIKE IT! SPIKE IT!"

Gabe leaned toward Chip. "What do you think of what Jojo said about Brent? Do you believe her?"

Chip put his glasses on to glance up to the top bleacher, then faced the court again. "I'm not sure."

"I thought we'd caught him," Gabe swore in a low, urgent voice. "I know he was hassling Leanne Heard at the arcade. I just know it! What I don't know is why. Still, I don't care what Jojo says about trying to save Leanne's job and delivering some message from his dad. I can't believe that it was all Leanne's fault."

Chip nodded.

"But I can't prove anything," Gabe agonized. "I wish we could just ask Leanne straight out. But who knows what she's really about, either. Plus, she'd never talk to any of us."

"You don't think so?" Chip questioned, his soft features taking on a dreamy look.

"Chip." All Gabe needed was Chip getting bogged down with romantic delusions about Leanne. Gabe wondered if he should tell Chip about the new gossip creeping around the bathrooms and the halls. According to the grapevine, Leanne made moves on all the guys she worked with at the Tucker Resort. Over the last day or two, the rumors had been spreading across campus like the flu.

"I just don't know," Chip sighed. "You can't believe everything you hear."

"According to Jojo, we can't even believe what we saw. What *do* we believe then?"

Chip shrugged. "Jojo's just as confused as any of us."

Gabe didn't know what to think, either. Lately he didn't even believe his own feelings. Instead of a knot, he was starting to feel like a huge hole had been drilled in his chest and something had been scooped out. And it wasn't just the loss of his show that was making him feel so empty. He'd found himself wondering weird things like what Kat saw in sleazy Brent that she hadn't seen in him.

But was that all that was making him so nuts, the fact that Kat no longer appreciated him? Was that all that was making him want to shout up to that top bench, *NOTHING FEELS RIGHT ANYMORE! I DON'T CARE WHAT JOJO SAYS. I KNOW THAT GUY IS A SCUZ, AND HE'S GOING TO MESS US ALL UP.*

As if to prove his point, just at that moment, Jojo went off the deep end, too. Midcheer, she smiled up at Brent. It started out as her normal five-hundred-watt smile, but then she seemed to forget what she was doing, as if Brent had put a hex on her. She froze. The rest of the squad kept right on kicking until one of the girls tripped over Jojo and another rammed into her back.

"Whoa," said Chip, referring to Jojo's pileup. "That was radical. Jojo never messes up her cheers."

"Tell me about it," said Gabe.

Luckily, the first half of the game ended with

the next serve, so Jojo could cover her bizarre mistake by pretending that she'd just stopped a little early. There was applause, the rustle of pompoms and the thudding of sneakers as the players and the cheerleaders trotted off to the locker room for a break. Gabe stared at the blur of girls running out of the gym.

"Gabe, you made it. How are you?"

Gabe heard his name and looked all around the gym before realizing that Amy Zandarski was standing right in front of him. Her bangs stuck to her forehead, and her face looked pink and beautiful from the exertion of the game.

"You came to see me!" she blurted out in her shy, excited way. Then she looked down at her sweaty uniform and gave her shorts a self-conscious tug. "Oh, thanks. I was hoping you'd come. Isn't it a good game? I can't wait for Saturday night."

Gabe just nodded, barely letting Amy's words enter further than his ears. He was still fuming over Kat and Brent and the disgusting fact that there was nothing he could do about it.

Three minutes into the midgame break, Brent was tapping his foot. His mind was racing. He knew he was finally on the verge of something thrilling, and he couldn't hold back any longer.

"I love that our girls' volleyball team is getting more attention than guys' B ball," Kat chattered. Then she stood up and hollered, "GO, LADIES!"

He nodded. At least Kat was beginning to be at ease with him, but she still had that please-like-me look in her eyes, the one he remembered from the Turnaround Formal. Put that all together with sports — which were his all-time least favorite diversion (*girls' volleyball, pulease!*) — and this might have been the dullest night of his life. He could only hope that soon he would have put in enough time with Kat in order to cover his reputation, and he could move on.

"Usually football is the only sport anyone cares about in this town," Kat explained. "We almost took district in football, but I guess you know that. What am I talking about?" She made a funny face, then played with that crazy necklace she wore. "Right, right. That happened just after you got here." She tilted her head and laughed. "I sound like Miss Grundy."

Brent managed to slip his arm around her and offer a warm smile. It was easy to put on a show, now that he knew this night wasn't going to be

dreary after all. He'd been worried after getting
caught by Gabe and Chip that he was really
going to have to watch himself. He still hadn't
found Leanne to tell her to keep her mouth shut.
But as far as he could tell, he'd covered his tracks
pretty well. Unless he had a public showdown
with Leanne, he was probably pretty safe.

Brent didn't want to think about Leanne. As
soon as he'd seen Jojo lose it in the middle of
her cheer, he'd known that some new irresistible
adventure was about to happen. Actually, he'd
sensed it on Monday, when he'd run into Jojo
while waiting for Leanne. And this new Jojo
complication was so tempting that he could put
Leanne on the back burner.

"I'm going to go and get a drink from the
water fountain," Brent told Kat, feigning a
cough and maybe even a hint of laryngitis.

"Bring me one," Kat joked.

He laughed and touched her cheek. "I'll be
right back."

Unable to restrain himself one second longer,
he shot up and walked down the bleachers to the
floor. Quickly, he crossed in front of the watching crowd and headed toward the exit. He passed
two girls trying to sneak Cokes into the gym,
then it was out the door. In the hallway there

was the cool, dry concrete smell and the double doors leading to the girls' and boys' gyms.

A few people milled around, no one that Brent was interested in. He walked all the way down to the water fountain, and there she was. Actually, he had the feeling that she'd seen him coming and had intentionally hung back to run into him.

"Hi, Jojo."

Jojo hovered around the fountain, finally getting up on her tiptoes and leaning to take a drink.

"I'll get that for you," Brent offered, pushing down on the fountain lever. The water squirted into Jojo's face, and she jerked back, crashing against him. He slipped his arm around her waist to steady her, then slid his hand all the way around her back when he let her go. "Sorry."

"It's okay," she managed in a breathless voice, barely able to get her balance. Finally, she attempted the fountain again.

He stood right behind her, pretending to be waiting his turn. Then he smelled her skin, the slight whiff of perspiration after her hard cheering. He noted with some pleasure the dishevelment of her hair as he blew subtly on the back of her neck.

She wiggled away, wiped her mouth, and offered the fountain to him.

He put on his most innocent, Boy-Scout smile, took a quick slurp of water, then accompanied her until they reached a secluded niche outside the equipment office, which had been locked up with a metal gate.

"So how are you?" she whispered nervously. "I saw you and Kat come in. You got here late."

Brent liked the off-balance, overexerted look on her face. And the idea that she was one of Kat's best friends made it so delicious that he could barely stand it. If only he could get Miranda, too, it would have been a perfect trio. "I had to do some work for my dad," he lied. "At least we got here in time for the second half." In reality, he'd been on the phone with some old party friends in San Rafael. "It's great to see you cheer."

"Thanks." Jojo didn't seem to know what else to say. So she smiled and did a little twist on her aerobics shoes. Her skirt flapped up. She started to leave.

"Jojo, can I talk to you for one second?" Brent asked in his most serious, I-have-a-terrible-problem voice.

She turned back, her dark eyes clouding with

alarm. "Sure. Of course. What is it?"

"Are you sure you have time?" He knew that anytime would have been a good time by the way she nodded her head. "I don't want to make you late for the second half of the game."

"I don't need to be back out there for ten minutes at least. What did you need to tell me? Is it about Kat?"

"Sort of."

Her sparkly eyes opened even wider. "What? Tell me. Maybe I can help."

"It's hard to talk about. I guess it's really more of a question, or sort of a request."

"What?"

Brent opened his eyes wide and stared into the light, willing himself not to blink even when the sting went across his eyes and into his sinuses. It was a great trick his best friend back in San Rafael had taught him. Sure enough, tears began to form.

Jojo stared at him, her mouth falling open. "Are you okay?"

He blinked once, then again, hoping to get enough this time for an overflow, a tear that would drip down his cheek. *Come on, come on.* Keeping his concentration on his eyeballs, he rambled, "I don't know what to do, Jojo. This is a mess, a real mess. I didn't ask for this to happen. I make it a point of never getting between friends, especially best friends."

"What are you talking about?" she gasped. "You're crying! Oh, no. Why are you crying?"

He swallowed and paused, as if it were hard for him to speak. "After we talked the other day, I started to feel so strange. At first I didn't know what was wrong, and when I finally figured it out, I tried to make it go away."

She was mesmerized.

"I'm attracted to you, Jojo," he wooed. "But I don't want to be. I like Kat. I really like Kat. But I can't be with her around you now. It's too dishonest. I just want my feelings for you to go away. That's what I wanted to talk to you about."

"Oh, my God," Jojo moaned. "Don't cry! Please don't cry. I can't stand it when anyone cries."

Now he needed to blink and stare, blink and stare while he tightened his throat and made his voice sound weak. "If it wasn't for your party, I could handle this. But Kat really wants to go, and I don't want to disappoint her."

"What do you want me to do?" Jojo murmured.

He wiped away his first drips, confident that more water power was coming down. "If I come, will you promise to keep your distance from me? Don't talk to me, don't look at me. And don't touch me!" He gasped for air. "I don't want to hurt Kat again." He suddenly decided to explode with anger. "I won't do it," he yelled, turning and slamming his fist against the wall.

"I'll do whatever you want, just don't cry!" Jojo yelped. "And don't hurt yourself. Please."

Brent held his hand while two more tears dribbled down. Then he stared at her, turning on the full force of his damp, blue eyes and opening his mouth just a touch. "Just tell me to go away," he whispered.

Now her eyes started to well up.

"Tell me I'm a jerk!"

Her mouth trembled as she tried to speak. But all that came out were little squeaks and sighs. Finally she flew across the few feet that still separated them, her arms groping around his neck, her fluffy hair all over his face. As Jojo patted his back and cradled his head, Brent decided she was the maternal type. She probably didn't know what a serious kiss was. He was kind of touched. And he wondered what he would have to do to bring out her nonmaternal side.

He wiped his tears and made a halfhearted effort at pushing her away. "No more. After this, we'll pretend nothing ever happened."

"Okay," Jojo whispered, nodding. "Please. I would never do anything to hurt Kat. Ever."

She pulled her hands away from him, then quickly got up on her toes and pushed her mouth at him. It was a knock-your-teeth-out kiss, so fast and hard and awkward that he had to do everything he could to keep from laughing.

"I'm sorry," she said as she backed away and put her hand to her mouth. She was shaking. "I just had to do that. I'll never do it again. But I've never done anything like that ever in my life, and I just had to do it. Just once."

"I just decided for once to have some guts, like I do on the volleyball court," Amy Zandarski was telling Kat. "I'm usually pretty shy off the court. But Gabe sure isn't shy. So I decided, what do I have to lose? I really like him. And at Jojo's party, I'm going to let him know."

Kat was having a hard enough time listening to Amy's heavy plans for Gabe, but when they both sauntered down the hall toward the drinking fountain, she felt as if she'd never listen to anything ever again. She'd left the gym and arrived in the hall just in time to see Jojo lunge at Brent. Kat was in shock. It was such a *déjà vu*, a recurring nightmare, that she felt as if the vision would never stop. For the rest of her life she would lie in bed at night and know that the only guys she would ever be involved with would be rotten through and through.

"I've been wanting to talk to you about Gabe," Amy continued in a low, determined voice. She pressed a towel to her face and glanced toward the locker room door. "He's kind of a hard guy to figure out, and you two always seemed so close. For a while I even thought you were a couple."

"Me and Gabe?" Kat managed in a fairly normal tone, even though she felt as if her guts had just been ripped out. She still didn't quite believe what she'd just seen. She tried to tell herself that it was Jojo's fault. After all, it was Jojo who kissed him. She wanted to believe anything rather than accept the fact that she'd somehow thrown away her judgment and her brains and fallen for another jerk! "Nothing like that was ever between me and Gabe."

"Good," Amy said with a grin. "I guess I wanted to make sure of that. I'd better go. I'm

sure the coach has some words of wisdom before
the second half."

After Amy left, Kat stood with her back
against the concrete wall, still not able to absorb
what she had just seen. Meanwhile, Jojo slipped
into the gym, while Brent was lingering, taking
a long, slow drink.

Kat knew she had a choice to make. She could
think about this over and over and go back into
her shell. She could confront Brent, decide that
he was scum and become a social recluse for the
rest of her life. Or she could go on. She could
blame Jojo and not think about the rest of it. She
could even assume that Brent was irresistible.
First Lisa had thrown herself at him, and now
Jojo. She could decide to just throw herself into
her fling with Brent and see it through.

"I can do it," she promised herself.

As Kat walked back toward the gym, she realized that she could never lock up her feelings
again. She couldn't dwell on her disaster of a
romance last summer and how she was going to
get hurt again.

Pulling herself together and holding back any
hint of tears, Kat marched back into the gym.
Refusing to glance at Gabe, she climbed the
bleachers. She could handle this, she told herself.

She would handle this. She wouldn't remember the painful parts, but would only feel the attraction and the thrill. Because if she accepted the fact that Brent was just another mistake, she might as well give up now and never risk caring for any boy, ever again.

TWELVE

"Please, everyone, sit down and get quiet. We're already running five minutes late, and I know how crazy you all get on Fridays. It's a wonder we ever get anything done in this class."

The next day Ms. Templeton threatened her fifth-period English class with the tip of her chewed-on number-two pencil. As usual, it didn't have much of an effect. Jojo was shifting nervously; Shelley Lara was going on and on about her date for Jojo's party; while Michael Foley and John Purdy were making their usual, gross, juvenile sixth-grade-boy noises in the back of the room.

"OOOOOKAY!" Ms. Templeton finally yelled. "COOL IT!!!"

She finally had everyone's attention and

slowly, almost begrudgingly, people went to their seats. Ms. Templeton pointed at them. "All right, class, you know the rules."

Creeeeak . . .

Over twenty chairs scooted. Ms. Templeton was a "circle" teacher. She believed in doing everything in circles, the idea being that people learned more when they talked to each other face to face.

"Okay, today we're going to be talking about the assigned reading. I take it that all of you did your assigned reading, right?"

A groan pushed its way through the classroom. Somewhere in back a tacked-up poster fell down, but no one noticed because just then the door to the classroom opened.

Leanne slowly padded in. "Yeah. So I'm late. Sorry," she muttered as everyone stared up at her.

Leanne quickly moved to her desk in the circle, which, as usual, was right next to Jojo's. Her lateness was so chronic that Ms. Templeton looked genuinely irritated. Leanne knew she couldn't afford many more tardies. But how was she supposed to leave the bathroom stall when the other girls were talking about her?

Leanne really goes after every guy she works with?

That's what my boyfriend told me, and he heard it from Brent Tucker!

I heard she goes after any guy that looks her way.

Finally the class got started, but when Leanne got through taking her book out of her patchwork velvet bag, she noticed that Jojo was looking at her out of the corner of her eye. Leanne wondered if Jojo were about to raise her hand and say, "Excuse me. Slut patrol. Please take Leanne Heard out of this class."

Instead, Jojo looked away with confused and strangely guilty eyes.

Lately Jojo said hi to Leanne. Usually she smiled, too, but this time Jojo was acting as if she wanted to crawl under her desk. Maybe she no longer wanted anyone to know they'd been on speaking terms. Maybe Jojo thought she'd get dirty just by sitting next to her.

"Hi," Leanne heard herself whisper first.

Jojo bit her lip.

Leanne doodled while Ms. Templeton had people read passages of a Jack London story out loud. She noticed other kids in class glance at her. They'd try to sneak in a stare, then look away.

Maybe she was just being paranoid, Leanne prayed. Chip had invited her to Jojo's party, after

all. Not that Leanne had ever taken the invite
seriously, or had even planned to go, but for
some reason that invitation suddenly meant
something to her. At least someone had acknowledged that she was more than a speck on
the Crescent Bay High landscape, a lowlife you
could gossip away about, never bothering to find
out if what you were saying was true.

Leanne had always been proud of keeping her
distance from other people at school. In some
ways she'd felt superior to all the rest of those
big-mouthed girls with their straitlaced lives and
boring hair. She knew that none of *them* could
ever survive on her own. But this time, they'd
gotten to her. She wanted to yell out, Wait a
minute! Just who's the lowlife here? Check your
facts, folks! Just because I never defend myself
doesn't mean I'm always guilty. She'd begun to
realize that when Chip had barged into the arcade
and yelled at Brent. Chip had stood up for her,
and that had made her want to stand up for
herself.

Remembering the concern and anger on
Chip's face, she started to feel bolder. Then she
felt a tap on her arm. Jojo was waving a note.

Leanne took it eagerly. Even though she
would have preferred dropping the note on the

floor, or throwing it away without even looking
at it, she was feeling too raw and needy to turn
it down.

She uncrinkled the paper as Ms. Templeton
droned on about the London story. Jojo's curly
handwriting in pink ink flowed across the page.

> *Leanne, I'm really sorry to not have let*
> *you know about this sooner . . . I really*
> *am. This is all very weird and last minute,*
> *but, well, I made a terrible mistake about*
> *the party. I didn't know, but my mom and*
> *dad insist now that I can only have so many*
> *people — about twenty. Would you be*
> *terribly offended if . . .*

Leanne crumpled the note in her fist. She
looked over at Jojo, who had her eyes glued to
the desk. Leanne knew that unless she jumped
up and grabbed Jojo, Jojo would probably never
look at her again.

Leanne almost flew out of her chair. Her legs
tensed; her arms pushed against the desktop.
Forget any of you! she wanted to announce. She
wanted to throw her books at the blackboard,
to leave that room, and be completely on her
own. Free and clear.

But deep down she knew that wasn't the answer.

A cold feeling settled into the bottom of her stomach. She took the note and tossed it into her palm like a tennis ball. Jojo finally did look over at her now. There was a real look of confusion in her watery, dark eyes.

"I'm coming to your party, Jojo," Leanne said quietly, almost as a threat.

Jojo flinched.

Leanne stayed with her. "I was invited, and I'll be there."

"Chip."

"Oh, hi, Lisa."

"Excuse me, I mean Charles. Didn't you once tell me that Charles was your real name?"

"Did I? I guess I did. But I hate the name Charles. Everybody calls me Chip."

"Oh. Well. Then I'll call you Chip, too. Funny we should run into each other."

"Yeah. Real funny. But listen, Lisa, I've gotta go. I just, like, wanted to see the new caf. I'd better get to class. See ya. 'Bye."

"CHIP, WAIT . . ."

Lisa was left with the echo of her own come-on voice as Chip's sandals *flap-flapped* away.

Soon he disappeared from view, and she was stuck peeking into their sparkling new cafeteria alone. Seventh period had already started, but it was Friday and Lisa only had typing, so she wasn't in a hurry.

While the quad emptied out, she snuck a look at the pristine white brick of the new cafeteria inlaid with mosaics of ball players and microscopes. The new cafeteria was at least twice as big as before, and had a special quick snack area and a nook for a new student store.

"Nice of them not to fix up this school until just before I'm going to graduate," she muttered.

In contrast to the new cafeteria, Lisa was still feeling like old news. She knew things were bad when even Chip Kohler, that wimpy sixties throwback, turned his back on her. Only a short time ago Chip had practically drooled on her high heels trying to get a date with her.

"I don't know why we even have to have senior year," Lisa complained. She pressed her face against the new window, leaving a trace of lipstick. "All the interesting guys are in college now, and I'm still stuck here."

Lisa was starting to feel like everything im-

portant at Crescent Bay High centered around
the junior class. Jojo was a junior. Most of the
girls on the dumb volleyball team were juniors.
Even the gossip the last few days centered
around spooky junior Leanne. And Eric, who
was a senior, might as well have been a ghost.
Rather than getting more energized as their date
drew closer, Eric just got mopier. He moped
over and over about the fact that he'd lost the
football championship and *junior* class president,
Miranda.

"Shock treatment is what's needed here," Lisa
decided. She left the new cafeteria and marched
across the quad, intentionally digging her heels
into the freshly laid sod. Ducking inside again,
she ticked off the lockers with her fingernails as
she walked down the hall.

Lisa was about to head for typing class, when
she noticed the activity bulletin board. Hoping
to find notices that proved to her that seniors
still had some pull, she lingered and stared at the
glass-covered board.

Her eyes scanned the notices. There was an
activity lull, it seemed to her. Someone was sell-
ing a motorcycle. There was an ad for Jazzercise,
a place to get discounts on movie tickets. There

was a special section for Friends in Need peer counseling, with a few notices stuck up in the form of privately folded notes.

Lisa started to walk away. Then for some unexplainable reason, she turned back again. She took a quick glance up and down the hall, then reached up and looked inside the Friends in Need messages. She wasn't looking for anything special, but she'd peered into notes on the Friends in Need board before and always found they contained something juicy, or at the very least, intriguing.

She looked inside the first note. A senior Lisa knew wanted to meet a peer counselor over a parent problem. Hm . . . A freshman Lisa didn't know wanted tutoring in math. Yawn. Lisa was almost ready to move on, when she saw a note addressed to "MJ." The printing looked distinctly male. Always more confident with anything male, Lisa reached for it.

"Jackson Magruder?" she wondered out loud as soon as she saw the initials at the bottom of the page. She didn't really know Jackson. He was one of those guys who, no matter what she did, never seemed to notice that she was alive. But she'd noticed him, with his attractive, superior air, and she'd read somewhere that he was one of the primo juniors in the Friends in Need peer counseling nonsense.

Lisa read the note quickly, then read it again, since the gist of it was hard to figure out. JM was meeting an MJ on the night of Jojo's party. MJ had been grounded, but her father was dropping her off at Jojo's. The plan was this: After her father drove away, MJ was supposed to sneak down the street, where JM would pick her up and sneak her off somewhere else. Then JM would get MJ back to Jojo's party in time for her father to pick her up again.

"What?"

The note ended with XXXXX's and other steamy terms of affection. Lisa understood that part perfectly.

But MJ?

JM?

Such a complicated plan just to leave one party and go to another without MJ's father finding out?

Oh, my God, Lisa thought, realizing that these initials were too cute for words and too amazing to be quite real. Jackson Magruder and Miranda Jamison. Talk about two people whose initials might match but whose personalities went from A to Z. And add the X's to it, and

you had a romance that could shock the whole
school!

And where did poor old Eric fit in? Poor old
Eric who was so certain that Miranda didn't have
another guy. Lisa memorized the instructions on
the note and carefully put it back. It was only
when she was finally striding to her typing class
that it all came together in her head, and she
knew exactly what she was going to do.

Time for a little shock therapy. . . .

THIRTEEN

It was almost party time.

Gabe was in Jojo's den, working on the stereo system while moving to a fierce rap song. In the kitchen, Chip was arranging nachos and dips, with a dishrag swinging from his belt. The sliding glass doors leading out to Jojo's swimming pool were open, letting in the strong breeze and sending clumps of balloons bouncing around the house.

Meanwhile, the hostess had locked herself in the guest bathroom.

Jojo stood nervously at the sink. In a ruffled pink party dress, she was stacking and re-stacking paper guest towels that had all been special-ordered in Crescent Bay High red and white. She wasn't ready at all. Since kissing Brent at the volleyball game Thursday night, she had practically been paralyzed from the smile

down. The one thing she *had* tried to do — uninvite Leanne to her party — had been done so
lamely that she might as well not have done it
at all. And after she'd done it, she even felt confused about *that*. Hadn't she once made a point
of being nice to Leanne? Wasn't her popularity
based on the fact that she was always friendly
and kind?

"JOJOOO!" she heard Chip holler from the
kitchen. Outside the wind pushed tree branches
against the house.

Jojo shuddered.

"Where'd you go, Jojo?" Chip called. "Where
do you want me to put all this food?"

Jojo didn't answer him. She swallowed and
took a deep breath. "Who can I talk to about
this?" Jojo asked her reflection. "Who can I tell?"

She blotted a makeup-stained teardrop off the
side of the sink and thought about the bizarre
situation. For the first time in Jojo's sixteen
years, she was the one with the romantic secret!
She was the one who had done something
scandalous.

"It's pretty windy out, Jo," Gabe hollered
from the den. "Maybe we shouldn't leave all
those lanterns and balloons around the swimming pool."

Instead of instructions, all that came out of Jojo was more shuddering.

"Jo. Somebody just drove up," Chip called again. "What do you want me to do?"

"Who just drove up, Chip?" Gabe called from the living room to the kitchen. "Is it Kat?" he added, his DJ voice sounding a little more strained. "Is she alone?"

Jojo looked at herself in the mirror again. At the mention of Kat's name, her heart had started to thump. Part of Jojo blamed Kat and Miranda for getting her into this mess. If both of them hadn't been so preoccupied and mysterious, maybe Jojo wouldn't have been so desperate to join their romantic intrigue club.

And yet, as strongly as Jojo now felt about Brent, she felt just as awful about going behind Kat's back. Sure, Brent had needed her. Yes, he'd been in tears, and of course she couldn't help if he was attracted to her. But *she* was the one who had kissed *him!* That was hardly a nice or a friendly thing to do. Jojo turned away from the mirror. She could no longer look herself in the face.

There was a knock on the door. "Jojo, are you still in here?" Chip asked, playing a rhythm on the door as if it were a bongo. "It was just your dad who drove up, Jo. He brought the ice and went back to his study to watch a video with your mom." After a moment, Chip knocked again. "Are you still alive?"

Knowing that she couldn't delay any longer, Jojo wet a guest towel and pressed it against her forehead. Finally she unlocked the door and met Chip on the service porch, where even the washer and dryer had been decorated with streamers and foil balloons. "Hi. Sorry to keep you waiting."

"Hey, I know how long you take to get ready," Chip said easily. "You still look good, though." He ruffled her perfectly arranged curls and led her back to the den.

"Thanks," she whispered. Then she walked into the wood-paneled den, where Gabe had just slipped on the earphones and was snapping his fingers to a tune she couldn't hear. The furniture had been pushed back against the walls, and the wind was making the drapes sway.

Meanwhile, Chip had shuffled over to the entry. He stood at the window next to the front door, which was made of gold-stained glass that looked like the bottoms of coke bottles. "Hey, look," Chip said in a happy voice. "Somebody *is* here. A guest-type somebody, I mean."

Gabe slipped off his earphones. "So, who is it this time?"

"It's not Kat," Chip said.

Gabe skipped a CD across the den carpet. "I didn't ask if it was Kat."

"Wow. It's Leanne." Chip smiled. "She really showed up."

Upon hearing Leanne's name, Jojo raced over to join Chip, kicking aside balloons as she made her way across the den. Hoping that Chip hadn't really been able to see clearly through the opaque yellow glass, she crouched down to peek through the mail slot.

But it *was* Leanne. She had just stepped into Jojo's circular driveway and was gazing scornfully at the driftwood sculpture and the well-tended lawn. Leanne wore a faded, baggy dress with an old fur jacket, as if she thought she was a movie star from days gone by. A gust of wind came up, pressing her clothes against her curvy body and winding her platinum hair across her face. No other guest was in sight.

As if she were having second thoughts, Leanne walked back to Jojo's mailbox and socked the balloons that were tied to the post. Jojo was still

frozen, wondering what Brent would say when
he saw Leanne. What would Jojo say when she
saw Kat? What about Gabe and Kat? Miranda
and Eric? Jojo and Brent? All Jojo knew was that
party or no party, her world of nice was falling
apart, piece by nasty piece.

"I think we might have one of those wind-
storms tonight that knock down trees and ruin
power lines."
"Do you, Dad?"
"Looks like it, Miranda."
Miranda stared out the car window as her father turned onto Jojo's street. The wind was
picking up, tossing trees and scattering trash.
But Miranda didn't care if her entire beach town
blew away; she just wanted this crazy plan with
Jackson to be over and done with.
At best Jackson's plan was risky. She was supposed to have her father drop her off at Jojo's,
then sneak down to the corner of Twelfth and
Holiday where she would wait for Jackson to
pick her up on his stepfather's motorcycle. From
there, she and Jackson would go over to meet
his newspaper friends for a short time, then Jackson would drop Miranda back at Jojo's in plenty

of time to talk to Eric and have her father pick
her up again. Just remembering the details of
their convoluted plan was giving Miranda a
stomachache.

"I'll pick you up here right at eleven," her
father said, glancing up at the streetlight in front
of Jojo's house. About a half dozen cars were
lined up. A handful of people were visible dancing inside the living room, and one girl stood
alone on the porch. Trees rustled, and the stir-
ring of the wind almost drowned out the party
music.

"Okay. Thanks for letting me go," Miranda
said, looking down at her jeans and red turtleneck. It was hardly the outfit for a party, but it
was the right attire for a night on the run.

"You think that Eric will be here?"

"I think so. I'll talk to him. Just don't expect
anything, okay?"

Her father nodded and finally turned to her
and smiled. He patted her shoulder. "I know
you think I've been some kind of ogre about
this, Miranda, and that I'm trying to tell you
who you can have as your friends. But that's not
it. I expect a lot, honey. I always have. And I
don't just mean good grades and school activi-

ties. I expect you to treat people in an honorable way."

Miranda fingered her diamond earring and looked away.

As she leaned to get out, her father added, "I trust you, Miranda. I love you. And I'm glad that we're getting this problem behind us."

"I love you, too, Dad," Miranda said.

As soon as he dropped her off in front of Jojo's house, she waved good-bye and stepped into the circular driveway. Then she waited for his Volvo to disappear, changed direction, and ran toward the corner of Holiday and Twelfth.

Brent's BMW whined and growled around the curves. Even though the wind was really blowing now, and branches were skipping across the streets, Brent drove as fast as he could.

"Do you know where Jojo's house is?" Kat asked in a worried voice.

Brent noticed that Kat was hanging onto the edge of her seat, so he drove even faster, down narrow back streets that were really more like alleyways. He braked suddenly when a trash can tumbled over and rolled in front of his car. He didn't apologize as he backed out of the alley and sped the other way. "I have that map Jojo put in the invitation. But I thought I'd take a short cut."

"This is the shortest cut I've ever seen," Kat said.

Brent stepped on the gas again. Since his success with Jojo, he'd been so pumped up that he was having a hard time keeping his cool. Plus, it was Saturday night. During the week he was able to keep up his Boy Scout Brent act, but since he'd been trapped in the small town of Crescent Bay, on the weekends he always felt like he was about to go nuts.

"You and Jojo have been friends for a long time, haven't you?" he hinted as he ran a red light and crossed Ocean Avenue.

"A long time," Kat confirmed in a tense voice. "A very long time."

For a moment Brent wondered if Kat might be onto him. He started to smile. If only Kat would turn to him and say, "You scum, how dare you lead on my good friend?" he might have stopped the car and really paid attention.

"Jojo's great," he hinted again, waiting to see if he'd get a reaction.

Kat stared down at her hands.

Brent turned up the classical piano playing on his tape deck. Then he swerved onto Jojo's street and saw the half dozen or so cars lined up for the party.

"That's the house," Kat said, pointing out a flat, ranch-style house with red-and-white lights strung across the roof. Kids were fighting the wind to walk across the lawn, holding onto their jackets, leaning into each other, and laughing as they made their way to the front door.

Now that Brent saw all the nice Crescent Bay High kids strolling into Jojo's nice house, even playing Jojo off Kat was starting to lose its appeal. But as he stopped the car and stuck his head out to feel the wind, he saw the one girl who never lost her bizarre appeal for him. To his amazement, Leanne Heard was standing alone on Jojo's front porch. Between the light and the wind and Leanne's bleached white hair, she looked like some kind of witch.

"I didn't know Jojo was friends with Leanne Heard," Brent couldn't help saying.

"Chip Kohler invited Leanne," Kat confirmed, shifting to look out the windshield.

"Oh."

Appeal or no appeal, seeing Leanne at the party changed everything. Especially considering that Chip was there. And certainly Gabe was there, too. Brent might be a thrill-seeker, but he wasn't a fool. He took chances when he could get away with them. But he also knew when to back off and cover his tracks. It was one thing to approach Leanne on his territory, but he had to be careful with her in public. After everything Brent had done to Leanne, she might just turn on him and expose him in front of everyone.

He suddenly faced Kat and took her hand. Slowly, he drew on her palm, as if he were telling her fortune. "Do you really want to go to this party with tons of people?" he wooed.

"Why?" Kat wondered.

Brent had the faint sense that Kat had cooled a little. But the sense wasn't strong enough to capture his interest. He decided to give her the final test. He'd propose something outrageous. If she went along, he'd be through with her for good. "I was thinking of skipping this party after all and going somewhere else where we didn't have to be in such a crowd. It's pretty early. Maybe we could go visit some of my old friends in San Rafael."

Kat took one last look at the party, then glanced back at him with those witty, insecure eyes. "How far is it?"

"Just an hour. If I drive fast."

"Why not?" Kat muttered. "I'm up for anything. And I didn't want to see Jojo tonight anyway."

Brent shook his head and began to drive.

FOURTEEN

As more people arrived, Leanne heard the squeals of greeting from where she stood on Jojo's porch. Music was blaring. Through the big picture window she saw a girl carrying a huge bowl of popcorn. Inside the den were balloons, banners, crepe paper, plus fancy matching furniture and family mementos all over the walls. All of it should have made Leanne want to step in, to join her classmates for once. Instead she stayed out on the porch, watching the cars drive up, while the wind tossed the bushes and the trees.

"This is stupid," Leanne whispered.

Entering Jojo's doorway felt like crossing a castle moat in one of those adventure games. It might appear to be bright and happy inside, but Leanne knew it could really just be a magic spell, one meant to lure her in so that the monsters

could appear. All the kids who hated her or
didn't respect her were inside — the ones like
Brent and Jojo who thought they could treat her
any way they wished.

"Come on," Leanne urged herself, "I have to
go in. Isn't that why I came?"

That was just it. She'd come to the party to
prove to herself that she could do it, and to prove
to everyone else that they were wrong about her.
She had her pride. She had self-respect. Jojo just
couldn't jerk her around like some yo-yo. She
wanted to confront all of them face-to-face.

Leanne finally gathered her courage. She patted down her hair, which had been tossed and
tangled by the wind. She wrapped herself in her
thrift store fur, crossed the porch, and rang the
doorbell.

The door swung open. A boy she hadn't
thought much about stood smiling at her, holding a bottle of apple juice. Glasses hung from a
string around his neck, and his long hair flowed
to his shoulders.

"Chip."

"Hey." Chip gave her his easy, comforting
smile.

She picked at her fur coat.

"I saw you walk up," Chip said in his open,

easy way. "I wondered where you went when you didn't come in right away."

"You did?" Leanne still didn't quite know what to make of Chip. He wore a T-shirt with some kind of recycling symbol and pants with tons of pockets. He seemed so laid-back and soft, but the way he'd tried to defend her at the arcade had definitely been impressive.

Chip stepped out onto the welcome mat. "This wind is something, isn't it?" he said, smiling and letting his head fall back. "Maybe you have the right idea. Who wants to be inside a crowded house when it's so great outside."

That wasn't exactly the way Leanne had seen it. Nonetheless, she took a few steps back, regaining her old position on the porch.

Chip followed her and slipped on his glasses. Then he sat down in an uncomfortable-looking lawn chair. "Look, I don't really like parties all that much anyway. How about if I sit out here with you? We don't even have to talk if you don't want to. We can just feel the wind and look at the sky."

Look at the sky? Was he for real?

Finally Leanne sat, gathering up her silky skirt and wrapping it around her legs. The wind ripped around, and the music played. Chip's hair blew across his face, and he just kept smiling and looking at the stars. Okay, Leanne finally decided. She could stick it out a little longer and look at the stars, too.

"Why are we standing out here in the wind, Lisa?"

"Eric, just be patient. You told me to handle the details of this evening. I'm handling it. You're sure this is the corner of Twelfth and Holiday?"

"Yes. And I'm also sure that Jojo's house is a block the other way. Let's go. I don't want to miss Miranda."

You won't, Lisa thought. Not if I've planned this right.

Standing in the parking lot of the Twelfth Street 7-Eleven, Lisa held firmly onto Eric's hand. In her short skirt and leotard top, the wind was going right through her. It whistled around the parked cars and tossed candy wrappers around the base of the phone booth. And the whole time, Eric — big and beefy though he was — wasn't doing a thing to keep her warm.

"Lisa, let's go," Eric repeated, nervously shifting in his cowboy boots. "Why are we hanging around a dark parking lot a block from Jojo's house?"

"Just be patient," Lisa repeated, clinging to his arm to keep him in the shadows. "You're going to take my advice tonight, remember?"

He rolled his eyes.

She grabbed him by the letter jacket and made him look right at her. Her red hair fluttered in his face. "Eric, my advice is, keep your eyes and ears open and just hang out here for a while. Trust me. We'll be on our way soon."

Luckily, Lisa didn't have to give any more advice because just at that moment the rumble of a motorcycle filled her ears. As the bike rolled into the parking lot, the door to the 7-Eleven opened, and Miranda ran out.

"What's going on?" Eric gasped, recognizing Miranda right away.

Lisa grabbed Eric's hand. He was so strong and determined that she was almost unable to hold him back. "Keep your cool!" she warned in a frantic whisper. "Don't make a fool of yourself. Watch and listen, and wait for her to come to you."

Meanwhile, Miranda ran. She'd seen the motorbike as soon as it had pulled out from Elev-

enth Street and headed toward the 7-Eleven.
Even in his helmet and leather jacket, she'd
known that it was Jackson. He was right on time.

Jackson put the motorbike on its kickstand,
then hopped off. Almost the same moment he
had his helmet off, Miranda was in his arms.

"I'm so glad you made it," Jackson said in a
bold voice. "I knew you wouldn't let me down.
I knew it."

She wound her arms around his waist, finding
a patch of warm skin under his heavy jacket. For
a moment she just needed to stand there like that,
to hold onto him and draw up her courage.

Jackson laughed and rested his cheek against
the top of her head. "Pretty wild night, huh?
Amazing wind. Are you ready?"

"I think so."

He pulled away to crouch down and unfasten
something from the back of his bike. "I brought
you a helmet," he said.

He stood up again and tossed her the helmet
in a happy, carefree way. For the first time in
weeks Miranda felt carefree, too. She caught the
helmet, then swung it by the chin strap and
leaned in to kiss him. She'd only meant it to be
a quick kiss, but he'd wound his arm around her

back and one short kiss turned into a longer one, and then another.

In the middle of the next kiss, Miranda's carefree feeling began to ice up. It wasn't anything to do with Jackson. She had the sudden, chilly feeling that someone was watching them. Slowly, she eased away from Jackson and looked around. And when she saw him, her stomach dropped as if it had just fallen off the top of a building.

Eric was standing only a few feet away, his straightforward brown eyes filled with shock and disgust. Beside him was Lisa Avery, clinging to his jacket. Lisa was biting her lip and was on the verge of laughing. At the same time, Miranda pushed away from Jackson and felt like she was going to be sick.

Eric came right up to them. His face was red and his eyes seemed like lasers. "You lied to me," he shouted, in a tone that was quickly changing from shock to anger.

Miranda shook her head. "Oh Eric. No. I didn't lie."

"You just led me to believe that there wasn't another guy. You made me think there was still a chance that you and I could get back together.

God, Miranda. You humiliated me once. Why
are you doing it again?"

Miranda looked back at Lisa. She was in
shock. Her brain couldn't come up with an
answer.

"Come on, Eric," Lisa cooed. She came up
and wove her arm through his. "Let's go to Jojo's. These people aren't even worth talking to."
She began to drag Eric away.

"Eric, wait . . ." Miranda called out.

Eric turned back, but merely shook his head.
"I don't want to hear anything else you have to
say, Miranda. I don't even want to look at you
again. You are dishonest. You don't care about
anyone's feelings but your own."

"ERIC!" Miranda called one more time.

Miranda watched Lisa lead Eric into the cross-
walk. As the wind whipped her hair across her
face, she realized that she was beyond tears. The
whole night suddenly felt like such a nightmare
that she wanted to scream in terror. This was
the exact opposite of when she'd run out of the
Turnaround Formal. She no longer felt she was
breaking free. Instead, she felt the world closing
in on her.

Jackson looked at her. "You told Eric you
were interested in getting back together?"

"No!" Miranda almost shouted.

Jackson looked unsure, but he put his arm out. "Okay. I believe you," he told her reassuringly. The wind blew his hair against one side of his face. "We'd better go, especially if you want to get back in time to fool your dad."

Her dad, Miranda thought.

She folded her arms around herself, then nervously touched her diamond earring. Her mouth was dry, and she felt as if all the air had been knocked out of her. How would she ever face her dad again? But that's what Jackson wanted her to do. That's what she *had* to do if they were to go out anymore. No, something had to change. Something had to stop.

"I'm sick of lying to people," Miranda heard herself say.

"So am I, Miranda. That's the whole point of this." Jackson tried to put his arm around Miranda's shoulders but she pulled away.

"I can't go with you."

"What do you mean, you can't go with me?" Jackson asked, looking worried.

She shook her head. "I just can't, Jackson. I can't take feeling like this anymore, like some horrible dishonest person who deserves to be in jail."

Jackson stared at her for a long time. Finally he took back the extra helmet and got back on the motorcycle. He tried one last time to reach for Miranda's hand.

Miranda shook her head. "I'm sorry. I just can't go. Leave me alone. I just can't." Her voice rose with emotion. "I'll walk home alone."

Jackson's hand dropped away. He started the motorbike, then he was gone.

Brent's friend's house was decorated with oil paintings and primitive wooden sculptures. It looked out over a man-made lake and was filled with collections of coins, records, teapots, hats, and antique dolls. But Kat couldn't appreciate any of it, because the collection of Brent's old friends was anything but noteworthy.

"Kat, I haven't seen my friends for a while," Brent told her after they'd arrived and toured the large sunken living room. He gestured to ten or twelve people stumbling around a modular sofa, tipping beer cans to their lips and lamely attempting to dance. Music screamed. Lights were low. Drunken laughter pierced the noise and the smoke was so thick it made Kat's eyes burn.

"Just mingle, okay," Brent added.

Kat reached out to stop him. "But Brent, I don't know any of these people. I came here with you."

Brent turned back to her and grabbed her arms, holding on so hard that it stunned her. He rolled his eyes. "Give me a break, Kat. You can't go through your whole life just hanging out with people you already know."

"Brent . . ."

Without another word, he left her alone in the middle of the living room.

Kat stood very still, feeling the music throb as people staggered and danced around her. Even though the drive to San Rafael had been over an hour, she felt as if she'd arrived in split seconds, with no time to absorb what was really happening. Now that she was alone, she tried to get her bearings. But the smoke was making her dizzy. The music was pounding in her head. Her thoughts were jumbled up with strong feelings of betrayal, anger, and fear.

She slumped down on the edge of the sofa and tried to think things through. As soon as she and Brent had left Crescent Bay, she'd gotten the terrible sense that she was in the midst of her biggest mistake yet. Brent had dropped all his politeness at the Crescent Bay city limits. As his

BMW had raced through the darkness and the wind, his gracious smile had disappeared. His refined features had started to look cruel. He'd driven so fast that it made Kat shake. By the time they'd reached San Rafael, he was barely talking to her.

But even then, even after Kat had seen that hard, almost crazy look on his handsome face, she hadn't said, *turn back, take me home, stop, no more. My brain is giving me very reliable signals here. I'm in trouble. This is bad news. I am on my way to my worst disaster yet.*

Instead, she'd still told herself to hang in there. She'd reminded herself of Brent's soft, slick kisses in the swimming pool. She'd told herself that she had to have faith in her feelings. Now she was realizing, however, that this was just like last summer after she'd met Grady and she'd gone back to his house. She'd wanted to say, *time out, not so fast, I have to think!* When Grady had started kissing her, she hadn't slowed down to catch her breath. Instead, she'd gotten lost in the feeling. Even when she'd known that she was going further than she'd really wanted to go, she'd been unable to pull back.

"I can't keep doing this," Kat whispered to herself as the party swirled and stumbled around

her. A preppie-looking guy stepped on her foot
and a girl spilled wine on her sleeve. Kat
wrapped her arms around herself and wondered
what would happen if she did say stop this time.
Would she just go back to being a recluse and a
joker? Would she never be able to take a chance
with any guy again?

Lifting her head, Kat decided to give Brent's
party one last try. She stood up and looked for
him, but she didn't have to look very hard. He
was strutting back into the living room, picking
up his pace when he recognized a girl who had
just stumbled in from the deck.

"BRENT!" the girl yelled out. She had a pale,
high-cheekboned face with straight, shiny hair.
But her lipstick was smeared, and one of her
earrings was missing.

"LANA!" Brent yelled back.

Kat winced as Brent charged across the living
room, picked Lana up and swung her around.
He greeted her so energetically that they both
fell onto the floor and laughed hysterically.

"So how's your new life?" Lana asked Brent.
"What's that town called you live in now?"

Brent sat back against an overstuffed chair and
pulled Lana across his lap. "If my father had
taken away my allowance for the rest of my life,

he couldn't have given me a worse punishment than making me move to Crescent Bay. It's his final revenge on me. It's this tiny beach town. It's nowhere." He threw back his head and yelled, "IT'S SO BORING!"

"How are the people?"

Brent cast the slightest look at Kat. "Hicks," he laughed. "A joke."

"Well, there are no hicks here," Lana giggled.

Lana fell on top of Brent and began to kiss him. Without hesitation, Brent clutched her and sprawled across the floor.

For some strange reason, Kat watched numbly, as if Brent and Lana were part of a movie . . . or a rerun. She remembered Lisa Avery. She wondered about Jojo. Her emotions were suddenly so turned off that she had to rely on her reason and her wits. And every thought she had was finally giving her the exact same message.

Brent was an incredible jerk.

His friends were jerks.

But the biggest jerk in the entire house was her.

FIFTEEN

"Gabe, do you want to dance again?"

Gabe peered across the coffee table at Amy Zandarski, who looked fresh and lively in pink-striped overalls and a lacy T-shirt. She was playing with a piece of popcorn they'd been batting around just a second ago. The music had just turned slow. She offered him a tender smile and big hopeful eyes.

"I don't know, Amy." Gabe tried to laugh as he retreated into the cushions. "It seems like I've been dancing all night."

"Come on, Gabe," Amy teased, leaning over the coffee table and trying to pull him to his feet. "Who else would I want to dance with? You're the one who wanted me to come to this party. And you're the one that I wanted to see."

"But I'm sure lots of other guys want to dance

with you," Gabe said. He tried to joke by playfully slapping her hands, then sank farther into the couch. "Maybe I'm just danced out."

Amy's smile drooped, but then she seemed to bolster herself for another try. "Well, if you don't feel like dancing, maybe we could take a walk instead."

Gabe shrugged.

Amy shyly gestured toward the sliding glass door. Outside the grass ruffled, and the water in Jojo's swimming pool moved in waves. "Everybody says it's so windy that houses are practically blowing down the street." She tugged on her hair and gave one last, hopeful laugh. "Don't you want to? We really don't know each other very well, but I'd like to get to know you better."

Gabe took in her innocent eyes again. He was beginning to realize what he'd gotten himself into. Amy was a good person, a gutsy, straightforward girl with the face of a china doll and the body of a track star. There was no doubt about it: Amy was great. But when he'd flirted with her so thoughtlessly — the way he'd flirted with so many girls — he never expected her to be interested in a heavy thing.

"I'm sorry, Amy," he said in his kindest voice.

"I guess I just want to sit here. Maybe I'm just partied out. Is that okay?"

For a moment Amy couldn't hide her disappointment. "Sure," she finally whispered. "I guess I understand."

"Do you?" Gabe made sure. He wasn't sure that he understood at all.

Finally Amy nodded, offered a sad wave and walked back toward a group of jocks that were standing near the front door.

"Sorry," Gabe said after she was gone. " 'Bye. I'm probably making a big mistake. I don't quite know how to handle this. I didn't expect it to be so confusing."

Gabe took one of the sofa pillows and hugged it. He hadn't expected most of the things that were happening at Jojo's party. He hadn't expected Kat not to show up. He hadn't expected Chip to spend over an hour just standing on the porch with Leanne Heard, then actually leave the party early to drive Leanne home. He hadn't expected Lisa Avery to arrive with Eric and tell everyone the shocking news about Miranda and Jackson Magruder! And he certainly hadn't expected Jojo to hide from her guests all night, as if her big party had turned out to be the worst night of her life.

Gabe sat for a while, moving slowly to the music and ignoring other flirty smiles and offers to dance. What was going on with his friends was all so complicated. He still longed to keep his life simple, even though he was beginning to realize that simple wasn't always possible because other people weren't simple. Certainly Amy wasn't simple, nor was Brent Tucker, nor Kat. Miranda had never been simple, and Jojo was getting more complicated every day. Even Chip was turning out to have some unexpected sides. And if Gabe really thought about it, he had to admit that he was pretty complicated, too.

Gabe was still thinking about himself and his friends when he heard a telephone ring off in the distance.

A minute later David Ronkowski, a senior debate champion, poked his head in from the kitchen. "Hey, Gabe!" David called out over the music. "Telephone for Jojo. Where is she?"

Gabe looked around the living room. The party was in full swing, revolving around Lisa, who was telling the story of Jackson and Miranda over and over and over. It seemed like Lisa's party now, since almost no one from Gabe's crowd was there, and hostess Jojo was still in hiding.

Gabe pushed himself up and went into the kitchen to answer the call himself. He picked up the phone. "I can't find Jojo right now," he said into the receiver. "Do you want me to give her a message?"

Gabe was answered by soft breathing and long-distance static. Music was faintly audible in the distance, as if from behind a closed door. Finally a hesitant voice came over the line. "Well . . . can I talk to Miranda, then?"

Gabe got that knot in his chest again. He knew from the first syllable of sound that it was Kat. Up until a few weeks ago, he and Kat had talked on the telephone at least once a day. He also knew instantly that Kat was upset and that she was calling from far away. "Miranda's not here."

"She isn't!" Kat pretended not to recognize his voice. "Oh, no. Can I please speak to Chip then?"

"Chip's not here, either."

"What? Why not? Okay. Um, how about Eric Geraci?"

Gabe glanced back to the den, where Lisa was hanging on Eric as if they were attached. "Eric's busy. Kat, would you like to talk to Gabe Sachs?"

There was a long pause. "Oh. Yeah, sure. Hi, Gabe," she mumbled.

"Hi, Kat. Remember me?"

"Hi."

"Kat, where are you? Why aren't you here?"

There was another static-filled pause. It was almost as if the wind were on the telephone lines, accented by a few rock drum beats. The knot in Gabe's chest tightened with worry.

"Well, um," Kat hedged, "I'm somewhere else instead."

"Did something happen with Tucker?" Gabe suddenly exploded. "What? I don't care how mad you are at me, Kat, you'd better tell me what's going on! I don't care how mad I am at you, I still don't trust that guy. If you need help, just tell me. Don't be a jerk."

"I'm not a jerk!" she yelled back. When Gabe didn't answer, she added, "Maybe I am a jerk. But that's none of your business."

"Says who?" Gabe pushed. "I'm sick of having you tell me what is and isn't my business. Why are you calling? Why do I have a feeling that this phone call *is* my business?"

"I don't know. I'm still mad at you, too, you know," she spat back. Finally she let out a long sigh, then admitted. "And . . . I'm . . . oh . . . okay. I'm in San Rafael."

"What are you doing there!" Gabe cried.

"Gabe, shut up and let me talk or else get Jojo on the phone," Kat threatened.

"All right, talk," Gabe grumbled. "I'm listening."

"Gee, thanks. All right. I came here with Brent . . ."

Gabe took a deep, angry breath. "I figured . . ."

"Don't say another word about Brent! If you start saying I told you so, I'm never speaking to you again."

"I didn't say a thing." Gabe waited for his heart to slow down. "So why are you calling?"

"I'm kind of stranded," Kat admitted. "I need somebody to drive out here and pick me up. Not you! Chip or Jojo or Eric."

"Just tell me where you are," Gabe said flatly.

Kat hesitated, then began reeling off directions. Even as Gabe was deciding whose car to borrow, he told himself that he didn't want to do it. He didn't want to go running after Kat. He didn't want Jojo to feel that another friend had deserted her. He didn't want to say good-night to Amy and have her know for certain that he'd only led her on.

But all that was too complicated. And the simple fact was, Gabe would have done anything rather than leave Kat stranded with Brent Tucker.

Kat sat outside the San Rafael house, watching the wind sweep across the man-made lake. Newspapers tumbled. Sailboat riggings snapped. Her mind felt like it might snap, too. She'd been tossed about all night, she was beginning to realize. She'd been thrown around by Brent ever since she'd met him. Maybe she'd been thrown around by guys ever since she'd started to date.

"Gee, I just thought I always just got swept away," she joked, hugging her knees and almost starting to cry.

Why did she feel as if she had to be over the edge, or else locked up in a box? Would she ever be able to join her quick mind with her heart?

Before she could begin to answer her own questions, she heard clumsy footsteps over the noise of the wind. She turned around, hoping to see Gabe, even though she had just talked to him on the phone.

It was Brent. He seemed drunk now. His hair was messy. One of his suspenders had come unclipped and flapped against his shirt.

"I've been looking all over the party for you," Brent slurred as he lunged closer.

"You have?"

"The party's inside."

"Well, I'm not," Kat said bluntly.

"Yeah. So I see." Brent rolled his eyes, then reached down for her hand. It was one of his old courtly gestures, made grotesque by too much alcohol.

"Brent, just go back in," Kat told him.

He knelt beside her and pursed his elegant mouth. "Aw, are we pouting?" he teased. "What's wrong all of a sudden? Are you mad because I kissed another girl? I guess that's just what you'll have to put up with if you hang out with me. I never said you were the only girl in my life."

Kat flinched. "Leave me alone."

He nudged her and scoffed. "Don't be a pain. Come on. Remember what a great time we had that day at the pool. Come back to the party. I'll be a good boy."

"NO!" Kat suddenly heard herself say as she scrambled to her feet. "I'm not going back into the party with you. You're drunk for one thing. And for a few other things, you're a liar and a sleaze. As far as I'm concerned, if I never see your face again it will be too soon for me."

"What?" Brent gasped, looking up at her with total amazement.

"You heard what I said," Kat told him in a loud, clear voice.

Brent still stared up at her in shock. Suddenly he crumpled at her feet, grabbing her ankles. At first Kat thought he was trying another of his charm tricks, but then he grabbed her so hard that he started to hurt her.

She kicked away from him, more certain than ever he was her worst mistake yet. Her mind was crystal clear. She didn't care if she spent the rest of her life alone in a hut, she was never going over the edge for a guy like him again.

"Don't you ever come near me," she threatened, backing away from him.

Brent got onto his knees and held out his arms.

"I mean it," Kat promised. "You are a total slimeface, and I don't know why I didn't see it before. You are scum, Tucker. I'm serious. I've given this a lot of thought. I don't ever want to talk to you again."

Suddenly Kat saw a new look come over his

beautiful, cunning face. His mouth fell open, and
his eyes looked hurt. Maybe it was shock, or
anger, or some kind of realization. Maybe it was
just the beer. Kat couldn't tell for sure. But that
stunned look was the last thing Kat saw of Brent
before he staggered back into his friend's house
and loudly slammed the door.

SIXTEEN

"So, was my party a success?" Jojo asked David Ronkowski in a bland voice.

David was in the kitchen stuffing himself with the muffins that Chip had baked hours earlier. It was late. Jojo could hear the party winding down in her living room. Slow jazz swayed. People chatted softly. Outside the wind had died down to a low, late-night breeze.

"I think it was a terrific party," David said, licking his fingers. "Where were you the whole time? I kept looking for you."

"Oh . . . I was around." Jojo shrugged.

"Anyway" — David grinned — "I had a good time. Great muffins."

"Glad you liked them." Jojo didn't bother to smile. Even though she'd asked David to the Turnaround Formal, he was definitely not a meaningful person in her life.

David brushed crumbs off his hands. "Well, I guess I'd better go. I have a big week in debate coming up. Thanks for inviting me."

Jojo nodded, still not believing she'd spent most of her own party hiding from her friends, as if she were a birthday girl with a contagious disease. Over and over she'd told herself to be the old popular Jojo, to get out and make sure that *everyone* was having a nice time. But each time she'd taken a step toward the living room, she'd seen Lisa surrounded by the rest of her guests. Lisa hadn't just crashed the party, she'd completely taken over! That realization had given Jojo such an unnice feeling that she'd felt as if she would never leave her room again.

Of course, Lisa was just the topper in a long list of nasty realities. Miranda hadn't even shown up. Chip had left early with spooky Leanne. And after Jojo had worried herself sick about facing Kat and Brent, they hadn't made an appearance, either. If it hadn't been for Gabe, her entire crowd would have deserted her.

Jojo stopped David just as he was pulling on his jacket and searching for his car keys. "Where's Gabe?" she asked.

"Gabe took a phone call a while ago and ran out of here," David told her.

"What! Where did he go?"

"I don't know." David kissed Jojo's cheek, leaving behind a speck of blueberry. "He just said it was important. He borrowed Shelley Lara's car and left. See you Monday. Thanks again."

"See you Monday," Jojo echoed, wondering if she'd ever have the courage to show up at school again when not one of her good friends had stuck by her. Not one!

Telling herself that she had to make one last effort at being the old Miss Congeniality, Jojo stepped through the kitchen door. She peered into the living room. But as soon as she was close enough to peek at what remained of her party, her heart stopped dead.

Lisa was in the middle of the couch, lying across Eric as if he were a mattress, holding court for the remaining dozen or so guests. "I don't know where Jojo is," Lisa was giggling as she sipped on a diet soda and played with Eric's sleeve.

Jojo backed into the doorway, out of sight again.

"You know how she is," agreed Jojo's fellow cheerleader, Brandy. "Maybe she's out inviting more people."

Guffaws.

"She's practicing cheers."

Side-splitting laughter.

"Someone said she's been in the bathroom half the night. Maybe she's working on her smile! Practice makes perfect."

After that, everyone — except Lisa — backtracked and said, but of course we all really like Jojo, and of course she's *sooo* nice, and *sooo* friendly and threw such a good party after all.

But Jojo just crept further away from her party again. The popularity queen felt like the loneliest person in the world. This wasn't just a feeling of being excluded, this was total exile. Her party hadn't helped. Her romantic interlude had only made things worse. Jojo didn't know what to do next.

Something in her life had to change.

The ride home seemed to take longer than an hour.

Especially since Gabe was driving Shelley Lara's old VW bug, which had no muffler and practically no seats. Kat managed to keep her balance on the lump of blankets secured to the passenger area, while Gabe used all his concentration to keep the car on the freeway in spite of the breeze and the engine's deafening noise.

When they finally drove down the Crescent Bay exit and onto Holiday Street, Kat relaxed a little. "I thought we were going to blow off the road," she said, finally breaking the silence.

Gabe patted the dashboard. "Nope. Trusty Gabe came through." He turned off the ignition, and they sat in front of her house while the engine continued to putt and ping. Meanwhile the wind was whipping down the street, banging the MCDONOUGH BED AND BREAKFAST sign against the side of Kat's mailbox.

"Safe and sound," Kat sighed. "That sounds good to me right now. Much better than out of control."

Gabe slumped down and tapped the steering wheel. "I know what you mean. You have been pretty out of control these last few weeks. First you go after sleazy Tucker, then you blow up at me — "

"Gabe," Kat warned. "Let's not start this again. You were the one who was out of control at the Wave. I can't help it if you can't handle having me date someone. I can't help it if the only way you know how to relate to girls is to flirt with them."

"Hey, I'm not the one who has the problem

relating to the opposite sex here," Gabe argued. "I'm not the one who had to be picked up seventy miles from home."

Kat suddenly felt the sting of tears. It was as if all the hurt and humiliation she had been holding back was suddenly coming up with full force. She turned toward the window, trying not to let Gabe see her cry.

"Hey, hey, pal," Gabe whispered in a much softer voice. He leaned over and gently touched her back. "At least you had the guts to give a relationship a try. Even if you did pick the world's worst guy, I admire that you went for it."

"Great," Kat began to sob, her whole body beginning to tremble and shake. "Because I'm never going to fall for anybody ever again."

"Yes, you will," he said, soothingly.

"No," she wailed, her voice echoing in the tiny car, her pain shooting up from the bottoms of her toes. She kept sobbing and shuddering, as if she would never stop.

"We all mess things up," Gabe assured her.

"What have you messed up lately?" she managed, wiping the streams of tears from her face.

"Lots of things."

"Oh, yeah?" she stammered. "Name ten."

"How about when I said I wanted to cancel our radio show."

Kat finally turned to face him and managed a tiny smile along with her tears, which just kept coming and coming. Gabe finally dabbed her face with his sleeve, then pretended to blow his own nose. Kat ran her hands down her wet face and pretended to flick water at him. Gabe wrung out the hem of his T-shirt, as if she'd gotten him soaking wet.

Finally Kat's tears slowed down. She took a big, shaky breath, picked up a Crescent Bay High pennant off the car floor and waved it. "Oh, well. I guess I should call it a night. At least I'm still alive. I got back home in one piece. That's some kind of victory."

"You did better than Jojo and Miranda," Gabe said, as he climbed out of the car and waited for her on the walk. "I think both of them might feel like real losers."

"I'll have to call them both," Kat sighed.

Gabe walked her to her door until they stood facing each other under the porch light. Kat wanted to hug him. She wanted to rest her head on his shoulder and thank him for still being her friend. But she couldn't get herself to make the move, so she punched his arm instead.

Gabe threw his arms around her, hugging her so hard that she almost couldn't breathe.

Kat hugged him back as long as she dared, then she began to dance. Sure enough, he maneuvered into a foxtrot position and danced, too. Kat jumped around some more, then tickled him. Gabe tickled her back, then pulled away and made a funny face.

"Hi, partner," he finally sighed.

"Hi, Gabe. Thanks."

He took a step away from the house. "So we're going to do our show again?"

"Sure."

"And you're going to stop picking fights with me?"

"Just like you're going to stop being a macho, pig-headed — "

"OKAY, OKAY!" Gabe cried.

"OKAY, OKAY, OKAY!" Kat joined in.

Gabe shot her one last funny look before turning his back and waving as he returned to Shelley's car.

Kat sat down under the porch light for a long time. She was glad she hadn't kissed Gabe, even though part of her had wanted to. She was glad she hadn't gone over the edge with him, or held back so hard that her feelings were locked up.

After such a terrible night, Kat decided that she was glad about a lot of things. Most of all, she was glad that she had started to use her head.

SEVENTEEN

By Monday at lunchtime, the windstorm was long over and the Crescent Bay High campus looked like it had been scoured. The freshman service club had swept the broken branches off the new quad, which was now open for use. The JV basketball team had picked up all the strewn trash and newspapers, and best of all, the new cafeteria doors had been opened, showing off an eating place that was sparkly clean.

But after the fourth-period bell, Miranda was walking away from the new cafeteria and toward the journalism room. In spite of her horrendous experience Saturday night with Lisa and Eric, she was starting to feel cleansed, too. Finally the bars were off her window. The chains were off her legs. She was no longer grounded, and she finally felt like a free and independent person again.

Climbing the central stairway, she realized what a weight she had been under, and what a relief it was to be able to move and talk freely again. By the time she'd gotten back home on Saturday night, she'd realized that she was almost glad to have been caught so that her punishment could end. She'd finally told her father everything, and her mother had taken her side. Finally, begrudgingly, her father had agreed to meet Jackson and give him the beginning of a chance.

On Sunday, Miranda had talked to everyone she could possibly reach. She'd talked things over with Kat and found out about Kat's horrendous time with Brent. She'd even called Eric, and though he hadn't breathed a word, she'd managed to apologize to him again. She'd called people from the Honor Society, the International Club, and other officers in her class. But now that her telephone privileges were wide open again, there had only been two people who had not returned her calls. Jojo. And Jackson.

Still, Miranda was feeling more like the old Miranda as she walked up the stairs in search of Jackson. She thought about the traits she had developed over the years that had made her class president. Her determination and leadership skills. Her courage and endless hard work. What amazed her was how she could be so good at that with her classmates, and then so lousy at it in her personal life. She *hadn't* really stood up for Jackson. She *hadn't* been a leader for their relationship.

"Dumb," Miranda whispered, "I've been in prison and it made me act scared and stupid."

When she reached the second floor, she counted off the large squares of linoleum tile. Just outside the journalism room, the noise and hubbub filtered out into the hall.

"HEY, DOES ANYBODY HAVE THE PROOFS FOR THIS LAYOUT?"

"Who's drawing the cartoon for this issue?"

"I need somebody to help me research Styrofoam."

"Are there any more spaces for student classifieds?"

Miranda breathed in the sound of purposeful school activity, something she had really missed during her weeks of confinement. Telling herself to be hopeful and strong, she strode into the room, her briefcase tucked under her arm. She spotted Jackson right away. He was in the corner, talking to an underclassman he was bringing up to speed on a school computer.

Miranda cut past the big metal tables where articles and proofsheets were being laid out. She walked up to him. She waited for the forgiving look on his face when he saw that she was greeting him in such a public place.

"Jackson."

Jackson looked up. But his smile faded the instant he saw her. Instead, Miranda saw that old defensive look in his eyes, the one he'd worn when they'd been enemies.

"Yes," he said, almost as if she were a stranger.

Miranda wanted the words to come out right. She'd rehearsed them carefully all weekend, even in front of a mirror. "I just came by to talk and have lunch here with you. Is that okay?"

She waited for his delighted smile, but Jackson kept looking down at the girl who was working the computer. "If you want to eat in here," he said flatly, "go ahead. But this room is really just for the newspaper staff."

His coldness went right through her. "Well, maybe you could come down and meet me on the quad," she suggested. "The new quad is really nice. Maybe my old friends will find a new place to meet."

Finally Jackson moved away from the computer and looked right at her. "It's too late," he said.

"But I told my father," she rambled, remembering her speech. "I feel settled about what happened with Eric. I'm telling all my friends."

Jackson barely seemed to listen. "Miranda, you know how I feel. I believe in facing things as they come along and shaking things up. Because if you wait and keep running away, then it all explodes in your face, like it did for us on Saturday night. I can't live that way, Miranda. I'm shaking things up with us before we just fall apart, too."

"What do you mean?"

"It's all over."

"Jackson — "

"It's all over," he repeated. Without another word, he went back to the girl at the computer and refused to look at her again.

Miranda stood in the journalism room until she realized that Jackson wasn't going to change his mind. As the words, "It's all over," echoed in her head, she clutched her briefcase and stumbled back down the stairs.

The new cafeteria was made of pristine, white brick. Everybody was talking about the fact that even the floors were spotless. Even the food smelled fresher to Kat as she stood in line with Gabe and Chip.

"Here," Kat said, digging some money out of the pockets of her shorts and handing it to Gabe. "I won't make you ask to borrow lunch money today. I figure I still owe you for Saturday night."

Gabe took the change, then reached for a tray and handed it over, pausing to wipe off the water splotches with his arm. "You're too kind. Maybe that should be a new radio character, the Too Kind Lady. What do you think?"

"I'll take it under advisement. All I can think about right now is how glad I am that I haven't seen Brent all day," Kat said, grabbing silverware and handing some over to Chip. "Of course, I've barely seen Jojo today either. Have either of you guys seen her?" When Chip didn't respond, she fluttered a napkin in his face. "Hello, Chip. Reality to Chip. Come in, please."

Chip tossed back his hair, then smiled and reached for a salad. "Sorry. I guess I was thinking about this weekend, too."

"So," Gabe teased, getting between Kat and Chip as they moved down the food line. He tasted different dishes as he stuck them on their trays. "What about Saturday night, dude? What about Leanne, latest and weirdest on the Chip Kohler weird-girl list?"

Chip nudged Gabe away. "Gabe, I just drove her home! Actually, I didn't even drive her all the way home, because she made me drop her off at the edge of downtown. I guess she didn't want me to see where she lives. Maybe I should ask her out. Do you think I should?"

Gabe didn't look so sure.

Kat rolled her eyes and paid for her food.

Chip paid for his veggies next, then led the way to the new tables. "I don't want to ask her out. Dating is so weird. Maybe I'll just run into her sometime, or hang around her locker."

"Maybe you'll see Jojo then, too," Kat suggested.

"If she ever unlocks the bathroom door and comes out again," Gabe teased.

For a moment all three of them looked around, disoriented by the new arrangement of tables. But then Kat spotted Jojo, sitting by herself at a big round table under one of the new murals.

Kat strode over by herself, leaving Chip and Gabe to chat with some guys from the audio-visual club. Jojo hadn't wanted to talk on the phone the day before — which was a fairly alarming sign. Kat wanted to tell Jojo that she knew about what had happened with Brent. And she understood. She also wanted to apologize for missing Jojo's party and to warn Jojo against Brent. She hurried between two freshmen and set her tray on Jojo's table.

"Hi, Jo."

Jojo looked up, but her smile seemed burnt out. "Sorry, but this table isn't available," Jojo said right away.

"What?" Kat laughed, assuming that Jojo was making a joke.

Jojo bristled and played with her yogurt. "I just don't want you to assume that this is our new table, or our old crowd's new table, I mean."

"Why?"

Jojo looked right at Kat. "I just don't want you to assume that I'm always going to be the one to bring everyone together."

"Oh," Kat said, a little confused. She took a deep breath. "Look, Jojo, if this is about your party, or . . . other things, why don't I sit down so we can talk about it?"

"I don't want to talk," Jojo interrupted, pushing Kat's tray away. "I've decided," she added, opening a fat book and setting it in front of her, "I need to be alone."

Brent waited until after school to go look at the new cafeteria.

He had deliberately delayed his drive home. He had no one to meet, no appointment with a school counselor or a student tutor. He was caught up on his homework (or at least the little homework he did), and there was no socializing he wanted to do after his drunken weekend.

No, this was a rendezvous that he was going to keep all to himself, an appointment for him and him alone.

He slammed closed his locker door. There were no books in his arms, but in one hand he held a heavy object concealed in a paper bag. He walked quickly. The halls were nearly deserted — Brent had waited long enough for that. There was still the chance, however, of running into one of the after-school crowd. A jock, a drama nerd, a journalism person, or even one of the teachers who stayed late doing lesson plans. Then there were the people Brent really was worried about: the janitors and the people in the administration. Brent hadn't been at Crescent Bay High long enough to develop a reputation with them. In fact, he'd gone out of his way to keep a low profile.

Brent didn't want to push his luck. Still, he walked swiftly, lugging the paper bag, knowing where he was going and keeping his mind directed.

It wasn't easy.

There had been so much to think about since he'd woken up the previous morning with a sick stomach and a throbbing head. The one thing that had pierced his hangover more than anything was the thought of Kat.

Kat had left him. She'd told him off. She'd actually found her way home alone, pushed him away and called him scum. No girl had ever done that to him. No nice girl, anyway. Never.

Brent almost couldn't remember the San Rafael party at all, but he knew that it had been a mistake. The whole night had been a mistake. Kat was strong. She was beautiful, and she had certainly proved that she was a match for him. Any boredom he had ever felt about her had flown away. Now he needed her. He wanted her deeply, fiercely, and he knew that the feeling wouldn't go away.

Brent pushed open the last door. He was out in the quad now. He felt the sea air and the sun, but it provided no relief. In a few swift steps, he was over a low hedge on the outskirts of the quad and heading to the new cafeteria.

When he got there, he peered through the glass and looked in. The brand-new floors sparkled. The tables gleamed. The brick walls were so perfect and white. Brent went around to the side wall that was farthest from the main building, but still visible from the quad.

Then he put his sack down and slowly removed the contents: a can of paint, a screwdriver, and a paintbrush. Quickly he popped the lid, realizing that he should have brought spray paint, but he was suddenly so preoccupied with Kat that he barely knew what he was doing. He stuck the brush into the blood-red paint.

Brent stood up. He reached out to the clean white wall with the dripping red brush. He stretched his tall frame and in huge strokes began to paint. When he was finished, the letters were almost as tall as he was. They formed one huge name:

Chip Kohler finds himself falling for social misfit Leanne Heard. He even persuades her to sing in the Crescent Bay High talent show. Will Leanne's next song be a love song?

Dangerous, obsessive Brent Tucker stalks Kat McDonough, determined to win her back after she ditched him in San Rafael. Kat needs protection, and Gabe Sachs is the perfect man for the job! At least *he* thinks he is.

Meanwhile, heartbroken Miranda Jamison is out to convince Jackson Magruder she's just as daring and unpredictable as the next girl. But how far will Miranda go to prove she's got guts?

Don't miss book #3 in the sizzling series
TOTALLY HOT!

LET GO

HANG ON

TELL HIM "YES"

PLAY HARD TO GET

TELL HIM "LET'S JUST BE FRIENDS"

HAVE A PARTY

TELL HIM "NO"

FIGHT PEER PRESSURE

HANG OUT

PROMISE TO BE FRIENDS FOREVER

ASK YOUR BEST FRIEND WHAT SHE WOULD DO...